MW01124659

PRAISE FOR THE NOVELS OF
KAREN FENECH

{GONE} Karen Fenech's GONE is a real page turner front to back. You won't be able to put this one down!" —NEW YORK TIMES BESTSELLING AUTHOR KAT MARTIN

{GONE} "Karen Fenech tells a taut tale with great characters and lots of twists. This is a writer you need to read." —USA TODAY BESTSELLING AUTHOR MAUREEN CHILD

{GONE} Readers will find themselves in the grip of GONE as this riveting tale plays out. GONE is a provocative thriller filled with a roller coaster ride that carries the suspense until the last page." —DEBORAH C. JACKSON, ROMANCE REVIEWS TODAY

{BETRAYAL} "An excellent read." —DONNA M. BROWN, ROMANTIC TIMES MAGAZINE

{IMPOSTER: The Protectors Series - Book One} "IMPOSTER is romantic suspense at its best!" —USA TODAY BESTSELLING AUTHOR MAUREEN CHILD

{UNHOLY ANGELS} "... a superbly intricate tale of greed, power, and murder... a suspenseful and believable story that will keep you reading into the wee hours of the morning. Highly recommended! — BESTSELLING AUTHOR D.B. HENSON

NOVELS BY KAREN FENECH

Betrayal

Gone

Unholy Angels

Imposter: The Protectors Series — Book One

Snowbound: The Protectors Series — Book Two

Pursued: The Protectors Series — Book Three

Three Short Stories Of Suspense: Deadly
Thoughts, Secrets & The Plan

SNOWBOUND

The Protectors Series – Book Two

KAREN FENECH

For Andrew with love and thanks

CHAPTER ONE

"So, how does it feel knowing you're taking your last ride?"

Mallory Burke didn't respond to the latest comment made by Hugo from behind the wheel of the sedan, refusing to let him bait her. He'd been doing his best to get a reaction out of her since they'd embarked on this journey into the Adirondack mountains of New York State a few hours ago when Hugo had discovered that Mallory wasn't just the new bartender his boss Billy Wilder had hired for his strip club, but an undercover federal agent.

Hugo had called Wilder with that newsflash and Billy had ordered that Mallory be brought to his mountain cabin—pronto.

Though Mallory wasn't responding to Hugo's running commentary, she was reacting all right. The gravity of her situation had her heart pounding so hard she wondered if Hugo and his associate, Miles Pratt, the other man in the car,

1

could hear it.

Pratt, seated beside her in the back seat, turned to her and smirked. His unibrow looked like a caterpillar crawling across his forehead. His large bulk took up more than his share of the leather bench seat, wedging Mallory in tight between him and the rear passenger door. The door was locked, though with her hands tied behind her back she wouldn't be able to open it in any case. She was currently working on loosening the knot, but Hugo tied a knot with the skill of a sailor. Lucky for her, she was good at untying knots. This one was just about undone.

The knot wasn't going to be her biggest obstacle to getting away from these bozos. When she did untie her hands, she was going to have to escape into the snow storm outside. As she thought that, the big sedan skidded and the rear fishtailed.

"Fuckin' snow," Hugo muttered.

On this, Mallory agreed with him.

Snow or not, there was no way she was going to the cabin. She'd overheard Hugo and Miles say with no small measure of respect—and fear—that the "Don" would be there. Though she wanted to encounter the "Don"—Paul Considine—with a fierceness that had her pulse pounding, she wanted it to be on her terms. Not like this. Not at Considine's mercy.

Mallory swallowed hard. Hugo and Miles had been taunting her with all of the things they would do to her when they had her at the cabin. Despite her professional training and years of experience with the Bureau, she couldn't hold back a shudder at the methods of torture they'd described that were specific to her gender. There was no way she could allow these two to touch her and, she had accomplished her assignment, found out what she'd gone undercover to learn and now needed to take that information back to the Bureau. The lives of twelve young women depended on her. Mallory closed her eyes briefly. *She could not fail.*

Wind rattled her window. Mallory jerked back, nudging Miles. For once, he didn't comment. He removed his safety belt and leaned forward in his seat. Eyes narrowed, he studied the near whiteout conditions. The wipers swished across the windshield at full speed, clearing snow for an instant before the glass was pelted again and covered.

"Slow down, man," Miles said.

"No way." Hugo swiped a hand across his mouth. "It'll be my head if we don't get her up there fast."

Fast seemed optimistic and foolhardy. They hadn't come across another car since Hugo had turned down this road. Apparently, others had the good sense to stay away today. Trees that lined this stretch of road swayed, buffeted by the force of the wind. Hugo's hands, inside brown leather gloves, were clamped around the steering wheel. He was trying to keep the car steady, keep it on the road, Mallory thought as the wind struck the sedan and the car veered off to the right. Just where the road was at this point was a guess. The thick snow clinging to the ground obliterated the road and it was only the line of trees that provided orientation. With the road conditions as treacherous as they were, Mallory might not have to worry about what awaited her at the cabin. She had a more immediate worry that she might not make it out of the sedan alive.

"We need to turn back," Mallory said. "We can't go on in this."

"Hear that, Miles? Little Miss Fed's got somethin' to say." Hugo met her gaze in the rearview mirror and bared his yellow teeth in a smile that made the fine hairs on the back of Mallory's neck rise. "Save your breath, sweetheart, for when we get to the cabin. You're gonna need it when you start screaming."

Mallory wanted to come back with a smart retort, but Hugo's words struck home and her mouth went dry. Work the knot. *Work the knot.* She increased the pace on the ropes to a frenzy, twisting and pulling. Perspiration trickled down her brow while she shivered with cold. Panic was setting in and she was losing it. Losing it was the surest way to get herself killed.

She forced herself to stop jerking frantically on the rope. Forced herself to fight back the panic clawing at her. Directing her focus to the task at hand, she went back to working the knot.

Miles had disarmed her, but she could see her gun tucked into the waistband of his black pants. Once she freed her hands ... done!

She was panting like a racehorse. Adrenaline pumped through her. She would have one chance to grab her gun. *One chance.* She blocked out the thought of what these two would do to her if she failed.

She glanced at Miles. His attention was all on the road. His shoulders hunched as he leaned forward so he was now perched on the end of the seat, clasping the head rest of the unoccupied front passenger seat.

"Slow down, will ya! I can't see nothin' but snow!" Miles's shout was barely audible above the wind.

Mallory reached out to grab her gun. The sedan went into a spin. The world swirled crazily as the car whirled like a top. Her screams echoed with those of Miles and Hugo.

The sedan struck something—hard. Mallory was flung forward. The seat belt cut across her chest, cutting off her breath but holding her in place. In a blur of movement, Miles was thrown to the front of the car and through the windshield.

Windows shattered, peppering Mallory with slivers of glass. She screamed. She was dressed in jeans and a jacket which protected her body but her head and face were bare. She swung her arms up and hunched her shoulders to protect herself from the spray of glass.

The sedan crumpled. The crunch of metal blended with Hugo's pain-filled shrieks and then there was silence.

She'd been holding her breath. She released it in a rush, the sudden surge pounding in her ears. She was alive. She repeated that thought and took another breath. Pain radiated from her right arm, leg and side. Her head hurt. When she lifted it from the seat back, her head swam and her vision grayed. Wind and snow blew in through the shattered windows. The cold air and wet flakes that struck her face revived her. She blinked quickly and fought back the blackness.

She wanted to get out of the car but was pinned by the front seat. The sedan had struck an outcropping of rock and the front of the car had been pushed back on impact. Miles's body was crushed. There was no doubt that he was dead. Given what she'd learned of his involvement with the twelve women, she wouldn't regret his passing.

Mallory shifted position carefully, testing how deeply she was wedged in. Not as tightly as she feared. Keeping her movements slow, but steady, she raised her arm. She gasped at the pain that shot through her, but took heart in the fact that she was able to move her arm at all.

Gritting her teeth, she levered up on her uninjured arm to free her lower body. Her breath shallowed and perspiration broke out on her forehead as she continued the slow, arduous process of extricating herself.

She was almost completely free when her ankle caught. Again, she cried out when she forced movement, but made another attempt, then another until her foot was clear.

That slight exertion had left her panting. She bolstered her flagging energy. Her cell phone had been confiscated by Hugo before he'd tied her. There was no way to get to the phone the way he was positioned. But Miles also had a phone.

She grunted and pushed the crumpled passenger door but it wouldn't open. Averting her face, Mallory reared back as far as she could in the cramped space and with her uninjured foot, kicked out the few shards of glass that still clung to the rear windshield then climbed out of the car. Outside, the blowing wind was deafening. Miles and Hugo had nabbed her as she'd been leaving the club that morning at the end of her shift. She'd already changed out of the mini skirt and halter top that were part of her outfit while she tended bar and had put on her jacket. She was thankful for that now as the bitter cold stole her breath and burned what felt like a raw wound on her head.

Her ankle balked at supporting her weight and she fell back onto the wide trunk. She needed support—a cane of some kind. Looking about wildly, she saw that improvising a cane wouldn't be a problem. Thick tree limbs littered the snow covered ground and she retrieved one.

Miles had landed a few feet from the car in a bank of snow that was red with his blood. As she crouched over the fallen man, she saw that his neck was bent at an impossible angle. He was clearly dead.

In the short time since she'd left the car, her fingers had stiffened from the cold. She flexed them and blew on them, then began patting Miles down. She found his phone in an outer pocket of his jacket. Broken. Unusable. She let out a frustrated sigh. Her semi-automatic was no longer in the waistband of his trousers. Likely, it had been flung away when he was thrown from the car. She didn't like being defenseless, but she was hardly in a condition to go traipsing into the snow drifts in search of it. It was all she could do to remain on her feet.

The sound of a vehicle approaching rose above the roar of the wind and then a metallic blue van came into view, glowing like a beacon amid all the white. She knew that van. It was one of Billy's from the bar. Her stomach clenched.

The driver met her gaze and his eyes widened.

Mallory's breath caught. Staying on the road was not an option. The mountains lay beyond. He couldn't pursue her into them with the van. He'd have to follow on foot and she'd have a chance.

Heart hammering, she trudged into the mountains. Her boots sank in the snow. For an instant, the tracks marked her trail but then disappeared beneath fresh snow.

The van slid to a stop. One door slammed. Then another. So there were two of them. Keep moving. *Keep moving.*

Her jacket was red. The color would make it impossible for her to blend in with her surroundings. The men would spot her easily in all the white. Without breaking pace, she removed it. She wanted to turn the jacket inside out and wear it with the liner exposed but the inner lining was also red. Her long sleeved T-shirt, though, was white. She dropped the jacket into the snow. She was cold and wet in an instant. The T-shirt offered little protection against the biting wind or the icy snow that soaked through the thin cotton fabric and left her shivering.

Snow crunched behind her. She glanced back. The men were giving chase, running toward her, overcoats flapping in the wind, slipping and sliding in their black loafers. The short distance she'd crossed had left her winded, but she increased her pace.

She had nothing to cut the wind that screamed like a banshee or the snow soaking her hair, her clothing and clinging to her eyelashes. She tucked her hair into her collar for what added warmth it could provide then huddled in the shirt. Particles of ice struck her exposed skin. Some of the flesh on her hands was cut from the spray of glass when the car windows shattered and now ice bit like tiny needles.

Another wave of dizziness struck her and she shook her head to clear it. She blinked more snow from her eyes and forced her protesting body to keep moving to increase the distance between her and her pursuers.

She glanced over her shoulder. She couldn't see the men now, but she could still hear them behind her. Hoping to throw them off her trail, she changed direction, moving deeper into the mountains.

Her side burned and each breath became harder to take. Her right leg had become a dead weight, forcing her to drag it and depend more heavily on the cane. Mallory suspected the reason she wasn't feeling intense pain from her ankle was because she was knee-deep in snow and numb from that point down.

She could no longer hear her pursuers. Hadn't heard them for some time. It appeared she'd lost them. Her stomach unclenched in relief.

She could not turn back and risk running into the men and she could not remain out here indefinitely. She needed to take shelter. She needed some time to think and she needed to find a way to communicate with the Bureau.

Focusing on putting one foot in front of the other, she moved on. Eventually, she came to a cabin. Her body seemed to sway toward it, but she ignored the yearning. Entering a cabin could be dangerous. She shuddered, leery of ending up at Billy's cabin. She would need to take some time to observe the place before approaching to ascertain that the place was not Billy's.

She needed to find out if the cabin was occupied. There was a large front window, but she couldn't risk exposure from it. A window high on the front door, devoid of curtains, would give her a view of the inside.

Her vision wavered. The snow looked fluffy, untouched up here, thick and welcoming like a blanket. The urge to just lie down on that snow, to sink into it, pulled at her. She shook her head. She blinked and took another step. She had to make it. Just a few steps more.

An overhang kept the snow from falling onto the porch but the snow drift had built on one side and was as high as her thighs. She waded through it toward the door, but stopped short of it, flattening herself against the cabin, letting the sturdy structure take her weight. She rose onto her toes to peer into the window. Her eyes rolled back. She fell against the door then everything went black.

CHAPTER TWO

What was that? Gage Broderick turned away from the frozen dinner he was nuking. Sounded like a knock at the door. Impossible. It was a blizzard outside, and he was in the middle of nowhere.

But the sound nagged. Ignoring the beep from the microwave signaling that his meal was done, he made his way across the rough-hewn plank floor of the cabin to the equally rough door and opened it.

A woman fell into his arms. Gage caught her against him as a cold gust of wind blew inside. Snow swirled in the air, the crystal flakes dancing then landing on the wood floor and instantly becoming puddles of water.

The woman was unconscious, wet, and so cold, goose bumps rose on Gage's own flesh from merely touching her.

The last thing he wanted was company. He felt a surge of anger at the intrusion. He had an instant—a flash—of just leaving her where he'd found her. He went still. He closed his eyes. It was a near thing but he wasn't that far gone. He hadn't completely lost his humanity. Yet.

He lifted the unconscious woman into his arms and carried her inside, kicking the door shut behind him. With the door closed, the wind was gone. More than the absence of cold, the cabin was again quiet other than the sound of the clock on the mantel ticking and the groans and squeaks of the old wood as he made his way into the living room.

He placed the woman on the leather couch and checked her pulse. Slow but steady. There was blood along her hair line. He parted her thick, brown hair gently and found a long gash at one temple that looked raw, enough to hurt but not severe enough to be life threatening. He probed further, but found no other cuts. He thumbed open her eye lids. Pupils were normal. Not concussed, then. He'd clean the head wound, but that was no longer his first concern.

Her hair was tucked in the collar of her T-shirt. Oddly, she wore no coat. Her face had little more color than the white shirt. He had to get her warm.

The snow on her skin was melting and droplets of water glistened on her face and in her hair. He got a towel from the linen cupboard and gently dried her skin, then moved on, drying her hair as best he could with the cloth.

Tossing the towel aside, he made short work of one boot, dropping it onto the floor, but as he tried to remove the other, it held. He ran his fingers gently over her lower leg and felt swelling in her ankle. Broken? He needed to free her leg. He estimated that the woman had been inside with him for about three minutes. She hadn't stirred in that time. Better that she hadn't. The way her boot had molded to her ankle, when he forced it, it was going to hurt.

With her boots off, he saw that her white socks were soaked through. He peeled them off carefully. Her right ankle was swollen, all right. Swollen but not broken, he judged and on its way to getting one hell of a bruise. He figured she'd had enough ice on that foot, thanks to the snow. Nothing he could do for it.

Her jeans were wet. Her T-shirt soaked through. No help for it, he was going to have to remove them. By the time he'd taken off the garments, he'd broken into a sweat. Not the result of shifting her slight body weight the few times needed to remove the clothing, but from what had been revealed to him. A tight, sexy body now clad only in a lacy bra thing and matching bikini panties.

Her underwear was also too wet to leave on and would have to go as well. Gage rubbed a hand that was no longer steady down his face then quickly finished undressing her. He yanked the thick blanket that was draped along the back of the couch and wrapped her in it. He rubbed her arms and legs to stimulate circulation, careful of her injured ankle. When her flesh took on a healthy pink tone, he cleaned her head wound and applied antiseptic. The bleeding had stopped so he left it to air dry rather than dressing it.

She'd slept through his treatment. He debated

rousing her, but decided against it. Her color was back. Her head wound superficial. Her breathing was deep and even. No doubt she was tired after walking up this mountain—and in a blizzard no less. The woman was lucky to be alive.

What was she doing all the way up here? Gage shook his head. Didn't matter. Not his problem. What was his problem was that she'd landed on his doorstep. He felt another burst of anger at that. *Wrong time. Wrong place, baby.*

The cabin was deep in the mountain and no doubt after the trek she'd just had, she was worn out. He carried her to the only bedroom, placed her on the bed and covered her with the thick down comforter. He left the room, closing the door.

What she needed now was rest. He'd leave her to it, let her sleep a few hours, then he'd get rid of her.

* * *

Mallory opened her eyes and groaned. Her head hurt. And her eyes. Part of the cause of her pain had to be the light streaming in through the uncovered window. Not bright sunlight, but daylight, and too bright for her nonetheless.

She turned away from it and the movement sent another jolt of pain to her head. She raised a hand to her temple and closed her eyes again at the hurt that shot up her arm.

Her head and arm weren't the only parts of her that hurt. She hurt everywhere. The biggest offender though was her ankle. It throbbed as if there was someone inside banging to get out.

Where was she? On a bed. An immense bed. In a room that could only be described as rustic. The furniture, the four huge posts of the bed, a dresser, and a chest of drawers were rough-hewn from knotted wood. The walls were a dark wood.

How had she gotten here? Where exactly was *here*?

She frowned. The last thing she remembered was stumbling across a cabin and making her way to the porch to check for occupants. She hadn't entered the cabin in case it was the one that belonged to Billy. Someone else had brought her inside.

She shifted position and then it struck her: Beneath the blanket, she was naked.

Someone had removed her clothing. The occupants of the blue van? Had she been wrong in believing she'd lost them in the blizzard? Her throat closed. Perspiration broke out on her skin. Removing a captive's clothing was number one as a means of intimidation.

It was working. For an instant, her mind filled with images of the horrors Miles and Hugo had described would be done to her during her interrogation.

She pushed her hair back from her face with a hand that trembled. Her brow was damp. Her heart was beating hard with fear. How was she going to get out of here?

She glanced to the window where frost glistened on the glass pane. Too small for her to fit through. It would have to be the door then. She firmed her lips, firmed her resolve.

She was alone. She didn't know how long she had before Considine sent one of his people to check on her, so she had no time to waste.

She sat up, then fought a wave of dizziness. She closed her eyes briefly, riding it out, then tossed the blanket aside. Goose bumps rose on her flesh in the chill air. Shivering, she left the bed. As she put weight on her right leg, she winced. She recalled being hurt in the accident. The leg could be a problem, particularly if she needed to travel a long distance on foot. Nothing to be done about that now. She'd do what she had to do.

Her clothes were not in sight. If she was going to get out, she couldn't do it wrapped in a blanket. There wasn't a closet in this room but the chest of drawers was across from the bed. Gingerly, she made her way to it, keeping her movements slow and deliberate to keep from putting her foot wrong and losing her balance, and to keep from making any noise that might alert anyone else in the cabin with her that she was conscious.

The clothing in the drawers was for a man or men and by the size of the garments, large men. There were a half dozen pairs of jeans all neatly stacked. She would need to fold the legs back several inches to be able to walk in them, but then she spotted a pair of sweat pants in a steel gray with a drawstring waist and elastic at the cuffs. These would serve better. In another drawer, she found a fleece-lined top and socks.

Mallory dressed quickly. She looked around the room for her boots, but apparently those were gone as well. Nor were there any mens shoes about. She went to the bedroom door in her stocking feet, and hoped she'd find her boots before she needed to leave.

When she reached the door, she stood against it. She told herself her only reason was to put her ear to the wood and listen for sounds in the outer rooms, but as she satisfied herself that she heard none, she remained where she was. She needed a moment to collect herself. Her breathing was rapid. Her body had grown damp from perspiration brought on by exertion. She felt as wrung out as a wet mop. And that was just from the short walk from the chest of drawers to the door. She was going to have to do a lot better if she intended to make it out of here alive.

She couldn't risk opening the door without knowing where it would lead. If someone happened to be in front of it, or was assigned to keep watch, she would give herself away. Biting her lip, she considered her options. She was in no condition to take on several men. Her only chance was to lure one of them in here. She needed more than her bare hands to take a man down today, and looked around for a weapon.

A large, pot-bellied porcelain lamp sat on the nightstand by the bed. She picked it up and flung it against the mirror above the dresser. The mirror shattered. Dropping to her knees, she picked up a shard of glass that was the length and width of her hand. Back at the door, she stood to the side and waited for someone to investigate the source of the noise.

The door was thrown open and a man ran into the room. She'd been right that at least one of the men in the cabin was large. Just her luck that it was a large man who was the one to respond.

Mallory seized his wrist, squeezed the pressure point, and twisted. She drove his arm high up his back then pressed the tip of the glass shard to his right kidney.

"What the—"

"Move and it will be the last move you make," she interrupted, keeping her voice low not to alert anyone else in the cabin.

Though he didn't utter another sound, his mouth tightened. She knew she was hurting him, but hoped her effort was enough to keep him subdued, because in her present condition, she wasn't capable of more.

"How many men are in this cabin?" When he didn't respond immediately, she applied more pressure to his arm. "Answer me."

"I'm alone here."

"Where are the others? Where's Considine?"

"I don't know any Considine. And, again, I'm alone here."

Mallory's breathing quickened. "When is Considine getting here? How much time do we have?"

"No one's coming. I don't know what you're talking about."

Mallory ignored that. "You're going to walk me out of here and then drive me off this mountain." Her voice quavered and she cleared her throat to force some strength into it. "Now, turn around. Slowly. We're going into the other room. If you lied to me, if any one is out there, you want to warn them not to try and stop us. I can and will—"

Before she could finish her sentence, she was flat on her back on the rope rug by the door with one-hundred-eighty pounds of male looming above her.

He pinned her arms atop her head. "Drop it!"

When she didn't comply, he pried her fingers open and the glass hit the floor. Mallory summoned all of her strength and brought her knee up, aiming for his groin. The man shifted at the last instant, saving himself from what would have been a powerful hit.

His nostrils flared. "Stop."

Mallory ignored his command. Heat emanated from him. She could feel his barely leashed anger and his barely leashed control. She bucked to dislodge him, fighting back with all she had in her. But he dropped his weight on her, pinning her with his legs, then he simply held her beneath him while Mallory continued to strain against his hold.

He clenched his teeth. "Keep this up and I'm going to have to hurt you."

Mallory stopped struggling, but only because her strength deserted her. She glared up at him. "I'm sure hurting me is the last thing you want to do."

His eyes narrowed and a muscle in his jaw pulsed. "Yeah, I can see where you'd get the idea I mean you harm, taking you in, tending to your injuries instead of leaving you where I found you."

"And what would Considine have said about that?"

"Already told you. I don't know any 'Considine'."

"Sure you don't," she said, making sure he heard her disbelief.

"My name is Gage Broderick—"

"Cut the act. We both know what's going to happen here." It occurred to her that all the noise they'd made hadn't drawn anyone to the room. "No one's come running to check on you so I guess you really are here alone. Considine left you to babysit. What are you, his stooge?"

"No one's coming. It's just you and me here."

His words chilled her. She'd been wrong about his role with Considine. If Considine trusted him to interrogate her, this man must be very good at what he did.

Mallory strained against her captor's hold once more and his grip tightened, not enough to hurt, but enough to leave her no illusion that she could get away.

Rage blazed in his eyes. "You're one hell of a piece of work. You attack everyone who helps you?"

Breathing hard, she said, "If I'd done it right, I'd be gone from here."

"Don't let the door hit you on the way out," he snapped.

Mallory frowned. "You look as if you mean that."

He grunted. "I'd like nothing better than to have you out of here. Believe it."

She stared at him, trying to read him, wondering what game he was playing. "You can't expect me to buy that after you brought me here.

Took my clothes."

"I didn't bring you here." He bit down on his back teeth so hard, his jaw cracked. "You brought yourself here. You collapsed outside my door. I took you in to keep you from freezing to death outside. I undressed you because your clothes were soaked. I couldn't leave you in them and risk hypothermia. That's the *only* reason I removed your clothing."

She *had been* wet from the snow. She studied him without blinking. "You don't know Considine? You don't know who I am?"

Fury flared in his eyes again. "Asked and answered."

He kept his unflinching gaze on hers. Was it possible he was telling the truth? Some of the tension in her eased as she considered his attitude. This man—Gage—really did look like he wanted nothing more than to be rid of her. That wouldn't be the case if he was working for Considine.

"Okay, Gage Broderick, if you really don't know me, then get off me."

He got off her, all the way off. On his feet now, Mallory got her first full look at him. Deep blue eyes, heavy-lidded as if she'd roused him from sleep. The snap was undone on his jeans as if he'd hastily donned them which reinforced her notion that he'd been in bed. The stubble on his cheeks and jaw was the same blond as his hair. He wasn't wearing a shirt and his body showed that the weight she'd had on her a few minutes earlier was all muscle. She realized her gaze had lingered too long and quickly looked away.

Gage retrieved the glass shard from the floor by her head while Mallory struggled to her feet. When she turned to leave the room, she glanced over her shoulder, watching him, but he made no effort to stop her.

Beyond the bedroom, the outer area housed a kitchen and a living room with a desk by the window and a large brick hearth that took up a portion of the wall opposite a black leather couch. The bunched blanket and the pillow on the couch made it a good guess that was where Gage had spent last night while she'd been in his bed. She scanned her surroundings and saw that they were, in fact, alone. Relief left her momentarily light-headed.

She needed to contact her office immediately. First order of business was to ask Gage to use his cell phone. She hoped there was a signal in these mountains. She had to get in touch with her superior and get the message about the women to him.

She also needed to get out of the cabin. She had to make sure Considine could not track her to this location and to Gage Broderick. The man was a civilian. Had no business being dragged into this mess. Mallory didn't want to divulge any information about herself or the investigation. The less he knew, the safer it was for both of them. The fact that she was even with him endangered his life. The sooner she got out of here, the better.

Behind her, Gage's footsteps struck the wood floor slowly as he also made his way into the living room. She faced him. "I'd appreciate the use of your cell phone."

"Can't."

"Mr. Broderick—Gage—once I make my call, I'll be out of your hair. I'll gladly reimburse you for any charges."

"The reason you can't use my cell phone is because I don't have one."

Mallory hadn't considered he wouldn't have a phone. "Okay. What do you use for communication? Whatever that is will be fine."

"I don't have a means of communication. No phone. No internet. No carrier pigeon."

Mallory ignored his sarcasm as his words penetrated. Her stomach tightened. "I need to get out of here. It's urgent. What about a vehicle? You must have a means to get off this mountain. For supplies."

"I have a truck. If you look out that window, you'll see that it's not possible to drive down the mountain now." He pointed to the window in the living room. "We're in a blizzard. Visibility is almost nil. The mountain road isn't plowed. I'd need a snowmobile to get out of here which I don't have. For the time being, it looks like you're not going anywhere. We're both going to have to deal with that."

He sounded pissed at that but Mallory wasn't concerned that he was less than pleased with her presence here. She had more important things to worry about. She went to the window and flattened her palms on the glass. Outside all she could see was white—and she couldn't see beyond the porch. Considine would have snowmobiles. She thumped the glass with her fist. The small gesture drained what little strength she had left and now that she didn't perceive a threat from the man standing opposite her, she slumped against the wall at her back, letting the wood take her weight.

"Why don't you sit down before you fall down."

Gage's tone was sharp and made her want to defy him. If she'd been capable of it, she would have. But he was right. Though certainly not a gracious invitation, she had no choice but to take it. The desk, with a deep-cushioned arm chair, was a couple of steps away and as she lowered herself onto the chair, she bit back a sigh at how good it felt to be off her feet.

She licked her dry lips. "Could I have a glass of water?"

Gage went to the fridge and returned with a bottle of the liquid. Mallory uncapped it and drank deeply then pushed back a vinyl folder on the desk top, clearing a space, and set the bottle down. She needed to clear her head. Splashing cold water on her face would help with that. "Washroom is behind the only closed door in here, I take it?"

Gage nodded.

A glance in the bathroom mirror showed her hair was wild and matted at one temple where she'd hit her head. Just parting her hair for a closer look caused pain that had her sucking in a sharp breath. Gripping the counter, and letting that breath out slowly, she took stock.

She was alive.

She'd survived the ride with Miles and Hugo.

Survived her frantic trek into the mountains.

For now, she was safe.

She allowed herself a moment to take that in but a moment was all she could spare. She needed to think of a way to get in touch with the Bureau and until she could she needed to take steps to protect Gage Broderick and to mount a defense should Considine or his people show up here before she was able to leave.

Bending over the sink, she washed her face. She found clean towels in the cupboard beneath, dried her face with one, then left the bathroom. The aroma of coffee brewing drifted to her but didn't spark any interest. She wasn't a coffee drinker. Gage had donned a shirt and stood sipping from a mug to the hum of the microwave. Boxes from two frozen breakfasts were on the counter. Though the smells coming from the heating food were dubious, she hadn't eaten since lunch yesterday. At the prospect of being fed, her neglected stomach growled.

As if on cue, the microwave beeped. Her water was on the desk where she'd left it. As she made her way across the room to retrieve it, she suppressed a cry. She was feeling the affects of the accident and every part of her hurt.

Her gaze strayed to the window. The blizzard showed no sign of letting up. Her stomach tightened as she thought of the twelve women and she released a sharp breath, ripe with fear and frustration.

She picked up the water and struck the folder beside it, knocking it off the desk. It hit the floor with a thud and a checkbook slid out. *Damn.* She went down slowly on one knee to retrieve the items. As she reached out to the book of checks, her fingers curled into her palm. The name on them was Mitchell Turner. Not Gage Broderick. Her breath caught.

She'd been duped. The man had given her a false name. Given her a false sense of security. Why go to that bother? Did he want to keep her docile until Considine arrived? Keep her from making a fuss or giving him trouble? Whatever his motive, his ruse had worked. He'd been believable all right with his *I want you out of here* routine. Cold sweat broke out on her spine.

Her thoughts raced. She had no weapon. She scoffed at the letter opener on the desk. She'd already proven that in her current state she couldn't overpower this man.

He was still at the counter. He didn't know that she was on to him. It was the only advantage she had.

She joined him in the kitchen where he'd begun his meal. Though there was a table a few feet from him, he remained standing to eat. An additional breakfast waited on the counter for her. The cellophane covering the food had been peeled back, presumably so it could be heated in the microwave. Steam rose from the bacon and egg combo. It crossed her mind that he could have tampered with her food, but she dismissed the thought. Why would he drug her? As far as he knew, she didn't suspect him. Added to that, he wanted to know what she'd learned about Considine's organization and who she'd told about that. She'd be no good answering his questions if she were unconscious.

A drawer that held cutlery was partly open. She got a fork and took her meal to the table. Now that she knew the truth about Broderick—ah—Turner, she felt sick to her stomach. She forced herself to eat, to appear as if nothing had changed between them, but her stomach had knotted and the food sat like a lump.

They ate in silence. He was obviously in no rush to begin her interrogation which reinforced her thought that he was waiting for Considine to arrive. The bitter thought tasted like bile. Her grip on the fork tightened. She forced herself to relax her hold so he wouldn't notice that she was coiled as tight as a spring.

He didn't appear to notice anything had changed with her. In fact, he hadn't even glanced her way. The man seemed lost in his own thoughts. She could relate since she was scrambling to come up with a way to make use of the set of keys hanging on a hook by the fridge. Specifically of the one with the SUV logo.

Her fingers itched to snatch the key, but it was still mid morning. Hours before nightfall when he would sleep and, snowstorm or not, she could try to make her getaway.

He finished eating then dumped his tray in the trash and the fork in the sink. He rubbed the night's growth of beard on his chin and without a word, left her alone in the kitchen and went into the washroom. A few minutes later, she heard the shower.

Mallory froze, listening to the water flowing through the pipes. She waited a moment. When the water continued, she pushed off the table and got to her feet. Heart pounding, she snatched the SUV key. Her boots were in a plastic tray by the front door and with her gaze fixed on the closed bathroom door, she put them on. As she eased the door open, she snagged her captor's thick parka from a peg on the wall.

Outside, the bright snow was blinding. She slipped on the jacket. It dwarfed her, falling to her knees. She pushed the sleeves way back to uncover her hands. With no time to waste on the zipper, she clutched the ends of the parka, and headed for the SUV.

She fought the wind as it pushed her back one step for every two she took. It really had to be the wind that was strong; she couldn't be this weak.

The SUV was parked on a short driveway on one side of the cabin, and was covered in snow. She swiped the sleeve of the jacket across the windshield but there wasn't time to clear the side windows or to dig out the tires. She could only hope that the four wheel drive was up to this challenge.

She got in the driver's side. Despite the wind, out here, without other traffic sounds, the engine would sound like a bomb when ignited, and she'd have only a few seconds before the man in the shower came after her. She stuck the key in the ignition.

Her door flew open. Her captor, dressed in a T-shirt and jeans that were already dusted with snow, yanked out the key. His blond hair was plastered to his head, dripping water into his eyes. Shaving cream lined his jaw. It would have been comical if not for the angry glint in his eyes.

Mallory scrambled over the console and out the passenger door. From where she now stood, she saw a window in the shower that had given him a view of her leaving. Her heart thudded. Her last chance at getting away had been blown.

They stood facing off across the hood of the truck.

"What the hell are you doing?" he shouted.

"Getting out of here. What does it look like?"

His expression was fierce. "You have a death wish, wait till you're back wherever you came from to fulfill it."

Anger cut through her fear. "Cut the shit! I'm on to you!"

"On to what?"

"You lied to me!"

"What are you talking about now?" he demanded.

"You lied about who you are."

"You're back to that?"

"I saw your checkbook, Mitchell Turner." Her strength was fading fast. Her words were becoming too spaced out. Being out here and talking to him was taking a toll. She only hoped he couldn't hear that as well.

His eyes bore into hers. "Guess I shouldn't be surprised that you went through Mitch's things."

"I'm getting out of here." Her heart thumped harder. "Back off, Turner."

"Mitchell Turner is a friend of mine. This is his cabin. I'm staying here. I am Broderick." He withdrew his wallet from a back pocket and flung it to her over the hood of the SUV. Without waiting to see if Mallory caught it, he turned and strode back into the cabin.

She missed. The wallet landed in the snow at her feet. She fished it out then wiped off the snow and opened it.

The man in the photograph was dressed in a suit and tie. His blond hair was shorter, but there was no mistaking that he was the man from the cabin.

He was Gage Broderick, all right. Captain Gage Broderick of the Washington PD.

CHAPTER THREE

Mallory stood staring at Gage's ID. Her grip on the wallet tightened. The man was a cop. A *Cop*.

She was no longer clutching Gage's jacket. It was open to the wind. At this moment, she needed nothing more than the heat of her own body to warm her. Rather than telling her he was a cop, and allaying her suspicion and her fears, he'd left her in the dark. She couldn't remember the last time she'd been this angry.

She fought her way through the wind and blowing snow back to the cabin. Gage was at the kitchen counter when she entered, a towel slung around his neck, coffee pot in hand. Gone was the snow from his hair and the shaving cream from his jaw.

Gage met her gaze. His eyes were dark with anger.

Mallory slammed the door. "You're a cop. Why didn't you tell me that? We could have been spared a lot of trouble." She shouted the words as she strode to where he stood, leaving damp trails of melted snow in her wake.

"Find that reassuring do you?" His eye lids lowered. His eyes became shuttered. "Shouldn't."

She'd thought she was as angry as she could get, but unbelievably, her anger climbed another notch. "What is that supposed to mean?"

He didn't respond.

Mallory crossed her arms. "Well, Captain Gage Broderick of the Washington PD, I'm Special Agent Mallory Burke, Federal Bureau of Investigation."

His gaze slitted. He didn't look happy about her introduction. Well, tough. She wasn't happy with him either. "Aren't you going to ask me what I'm doing here?"

"No." His jaw clenched. "All I'm interested in is getting you out of here."

Mallory was fuming. Though her mistaking him for one of Considine's people was his fault since he hadn't identified himself, it looked like it was up to her to explain the gravity of their situation and—though it left a sour taste in her mouth—to extend the olive branch. Tamping down on her anger, she decided to try a different approach. She removed her boots and replaced his jacket on the peg. Pushing the hair that had become wet from the snow back from her brow, she joined him at the counter.

"You're on vacation." That was the only reason she could think for him being up here. Though she preferred a white sand beach and a Caribbean sun, to each his own. "Look, I get that and I'm sorry to crash your R and R." And she was. She knew how important down time was in their line of work. "Now that I have, though, I'll bring you up to speed on how I ended up here—"

"Don't."

"You don't understand—"

His pupils darkened. "I don't care how you came to be here. As soon as the snow lets up, I'll get you off this mountain and into town. You can forget you were ever here. That's what I intend to do."

Mallory struggled for calm. "Look—"

"No. You look." He set the pot down on the counter with a thump. "First you jump me and try to stab me, and now you try to steal my truck. Like I said before, you're some piece of work, Burke."

Mallory's anger flared. "The reason I jumped you and tried to drive out of here just now was because I thought you were working for the man I'm investigating. Does the name Paul Considine mean anything to you?"

"You already dropped that name and I told you, never heard of him."

"Paul Considine is a crime lord. He knows that I'm on to him. He's looking for me. When he finds me here, he'll kill me and now, you, too."

Gage eyes blazed. "Just what the hell are you into for the Feds?"

"I was looking into the disappearance of a nineteen-year-old woman."

Gage crossed his arms. "The FBI doesn't investigate missing persons cases."

"The investigation started out unofficial. I follow missing persons cases involving young women."

Gage's gaze grew intent. Hers was the kind of response that sparked more questions, but he didn't press her for clarification, maybe wanting her to get the entire story out. Whatever his reason, she was glad. She had no intention of sharing that part of her life with him.

"The day before the woman vanished," Mallory went on, "she'd been seen at a strip club. When local police questioned the club manager, he said that the girl had come in looking for a job as a dancer, but had been turned away because she wasn't talented. That would have been the end of it, but I found out that another woman, one year older, who had disappeared a few months earlier, had also been at that club."

Mallory rubbed her forehead. "I went to my superior with what I'd learned. He agreed that the connection between the women's disappearance at the club was worth pursuing so I got a job there tending bar. I found out that twelve women had been abducted over a period of three months and are being held, awaiting transport out of the country. The club is a front for human traffickers."

Gage's mouth tightened.

Mallory laced her fingers in a fierce grip. "I found out where the women are being kept, but haven't had a chance to take that information back to the Bureau. The trafficking operation is run by a man known only as the 'Don' but I believe the Don to be Paul Considine, a local organized crime boss."

Gage swore under his breath. "How did you get

on Considine's radar?"

"My cover was blown." She shook her head slowly. "I don't know how that happened. I got away before he could question me about what I learned of his operation and made my way here." She fixed Gage with a look. "I know you said you'd get me out of here when the storm ends but by now Considine is tracking me. He'll have a fleet of snowmobiles. He will find me. That's a given. It's only a matter of when." A chill went through her and she hugged herself.

Gage went to the kitchen and took his service revolver from one of the drawers along with spare ammunition. He stood looking at the bullets then exhaled a deep breath.

Mallory could see there weren't many. "Is that all the ammo you have?"

"Yeah." He closed his fist around the few additional rounds. "We need to see what we have around here that can be used as a weapon."

He went to the door and put on his parka.

Mallory gaped at him. "What are you doing?"

He reached for his boots. "What does it look like?"

"It looks like you're going outside."

"A gold star for you."

Mallory crossed the room to where he stood, doing all she could to keep from dragging her injured leg. "Haven't you been listening to what I said about Considine? His people could be out there, watching this place. Waiting to make a move."

"The snow hasn't let up. Visibility is still almost nil. And it's light out. If you were going to make a move on us, wouldn't you wait until dark?"

Mallory chewed her lip. She and Gage would be at their most vulnerable at night. Considine would take that advantage. She nodded.

"You take a look in here," Gage said. "I'll see what I can scrounge up outside. I have a flare gun in the back of the truck for emergencies. There's a shed out back. I'll see if there's anything in there we can use." He picked up the shovel that was beside the hearth.

No doubt he'd need to dig out the door to the shed before he could get inside. He'd be out there for a while. Mallory rubbed her forehead. She was torn between wanting the flare gun and anything else Gage could find and concern for his safety. Added to the threat of Considine, was the lack of visibility and the snow drifts that presented another form of danger. "Should we tie a rope around your waist so you'll be able to find your way back here?"

"Not necessary. The shed's not far. I'll be right back."

He opened the door, letting in a gust of air so cold, Mallory sucked in a breath. With her arms wrapped around herself, she went into the kitchen to begin her own search. Under the sink, she found a fire extinguisher. In a drawer, were a couple of wicked kitchen knives. The knives and extinguisher could only be used if Considine was in close. As she gathered the items, she hoped he wouldn't have the chance to get that close.

How much time had passed since Gage left? She couldn't read the time from where she stood and returned to the living area. As she watched the hands on the small clock on the mantel move around the dial, she didn't think the man had an understanding of "right back". She'd heard of ranchers venturing out during snow storms and becoming disoriented and lost within a few steps. Just how 'out back' was the shed?

She went to the window in the bedroom that overlooked the back of this property. Wiping her sleeve against the window did nothing more than make her arm cold. With the blowing snow, she certainly couldn't see a shed, or Gage.

Back in the living area, she looked around the cabin for rope. She found some coiled in a crate beside the hearth, atop a mountain of firewood. When twenty seven minutes had gone by, and Gage still hadn't returned, she decided enough time had passed. She tied the rope to a support post. Tugging on it, she deemed it secure. As she put on her boots, she wished she still had her jacket.

She was tying the rope around her waist when the door swung inward. Gage, covered in snow, stood on the threshold. She never thought she'd say this about him, but she was thrilled to see him. Mallory stepped back to allow him to enter.

His movements were a little measured, a little stiff as he made his way inside. He set the items he'd brought back with him on the floor. In addition to the flare gun, he'd returned with additional flares, a spool of fence wire, wire cutters, and a can of gasoline.

He paused, taking off one glove and pointed to the rope at her waist. "What are you doing? Don't tell me you were thinking of going outside?"

"I was doing more than thinking about it. You've been gone for almost half an hour. I was afraid you'd gotten lost in the storm."

"So you were—what—going to pull a rescue?"

At his tone, she raised an eyebrow. "Yeah, I was."

"That would have been a fool thing to do."

Mallory bristled. "Really?"

"Yeah, really. While I know my way around this place, you don't. You would have surely gotten lost and when I got back here, I would have had to go back out looking for you."

Mallory lifted her brows. "Well, put that way, what an inconvenience that would have been for you. I'm glad I didn't attempt it." Her voice dripped sarcasm.

"That makes two of us."

Granted he had not seen her at her best since they'd met, but she was intelligent and competent. To join the Bureau, she'd been required to pass similar tests to what had been required of him for the police force, including physical and endurance tests and she resented his attitude that she was incapable.

Gage unlaced his boots, then went into the kitchen and set the items on the table. He shrugged out of his parka and slung it over a chair.

Putting aside her resentment for the moment, she focused on mounting their defense against Considine. "What's the plan?"

"We're making bombs."

"What can I do to help?"

Gage picked up the towel on the counter that he'd used after Mallory's attempt to leave in his truck and dried his face and hair. "There are a few bottles of beer in the fridge. Would you get them? Look for glass bottles or jars as well."

A few moments later, she closed the fridge door and placed the bottles on the kitchen table. She moved to the pantry cupboard and dug out a jar of spaghetti sauce which she held up.

Gage nodded. "Five in total. Empty them and hand them to me, would you?"

She poured the beer into the sink, then passed the empties to Gage. The sauce went next.

Gage poured gasoline into them. The smells of beer and tomato sauce and the odor of gasoline hung in the air.

When he finished filling the bottles and the jar with the gas, he put his parka on again. "I'm going to plant these."

"I'll give you a hand."

He shook his head. "Would be rough going in the snow with that foot. I'll do this."

Since Miles and Hugo had put her in their car, Mallory felt as if her life was spinning out of control and there was nothing she could do about it. She needed to do something to regain that control. She had no intention of blurting that out to Gage. Instead she said, "I'll be fine. I want to help."

Gage studied her for a moment, then took his parka from the back of the chair and held it out to her. "Put this on."

"What about you?"

"Mitch left one in the hall closet."

Gage returned wearing the extra parka and they left the cabin. The wind shrieked, overriding all other sound. Though Gage was only a couple of feet in front of her, she couldn't make him out in the blowing snow. It was only when he stopped moving, and she caught right up to him that he became visible again.

Blinking snow from her eyes, Mallory watched as he went about setting the bottles at intervals beneath the Evergreens that grew beyond the cabin. He was establishing a pattern, she realized, placing a bottle beneath each third tree, beginning with the first one in the line, so they'd know where each of the crude bombs was. Then, he dug a hole in the snow to both anchor and conceal a bottle.

Mallory flexed her fingers in the over-sized gloves that had been in the jacket pockets then held out her hand to Gage. He handed one of the bottles to her. She crouched and did as he had.

After they'd finished, he stepped back, surveying their work. The bottles were well hidden in the snow.

"Someone who doesn't know where to look for them, won't spot them." Mallory raised her voice to be heard above the wind.

"Agreed."

He unwound the spool of wire, cut a length, then strung it between two trees about four feet up from the ground. He repeated this several times, stringing wire between other pairs of trees that grew around the cabin. Whoever came through those trees first would be pulled off the snowmobile. At high speed, the result could be fatal. There was not enough wire for the entire perimeter, and large gaps leading to the cabin remained. Gage pocketed the now empty spool.

Back in the cabin, he tossed the spool into the trash. "If necessary, we'll use my gun to take out Considine's men and to set off those charges."

But his expression was grim and she believed he was thinking as she was, they had Gage's service revolver with limited ammo, five home made bombs, and six flares, not enough to provide the fire power they'd need against Considine and the contingent of men he'd bring with him.

After they'd removed their outerwear and dried off from the snow, Gage placed his weapon at the small of his back and went about the cabin, drawing curtains. Over the window on the front door which had no covering, he tacked up a towel. As the outside world disappeared, Mallory felt as if she were being entombed and her breaths shortened. Necessary, she told herself to cloak the windows, and worked to regulate her breathing.

Gage secured their environment as best he could. But the cabin hadn't been designed to be a fort and his efforts at reinforcement were limited. By late afternoon, they'd done all they could and Mallory feared that the only real chance they had was to be gone from here before Considine found them.

Mallory linked her fingers. "How long do you think it will be before we can get off this mountain? How long do snow storms up here typically last?"

"No idea."

"Didn't you look into what the weather was expected to be like before you decided to vacation up here?"

"Never said I was on vacation."

"Then what are you doing up here?"

Without responding, he brushed by her, effectively dismissing her. For the second time that day, Mallory was left to stare after him as he returned to the kitchen. If they'd been anywhere but there she would have walked away from him and never looked back. Just what kind of cop was he? What kind of police captain?

At the window, she pushed aside the drape slightly and noted that the whiteout condition hadn't eased. If anything, it was snowing harder. Visibility had worsened in the minutes since they'd returned to the cabin from planting the bombs, but Considine would not let the weather stop him.

While the weather now kept her imprisoned as surely as Considine would, the clock was ticking for the women. Worry struck Mallory again and she railed at the snow.

Her shoulders slumped and while the constant sparring with Gage had sapped the last of her energy, the fault for her fatigue wasn't entirely his. The last eighteen hours had taken a toll. She felt as weak as a kitten. Her head was pounding, her side ached, and she felt as if an anvil was on her chest.

She went to the bathroom in search of pain reliever and to assess her injuries. When she removed the sweat shirt she'd taken from Gage, she saw why she hurt. Her reflection showed deep bruises where the seatbelt had cut across her chest and where her body must have struck the door during the accident. At the very least, she needed a cold compress. As it was now, she could hardly move from the pain.

Passing on the aspirin for the moment, she took a wash cloth from the cupboard beneath the sink, and soaked it with cold water. She pressed the cloth to her chest and sighed as some of the pain subsided.

Soaking the cloth again and again, she pressed it to the various bruises on the front of her body. No matter how hard she tried, though, she couldn't get to the bruises on her back.

"You've been in there for thirty minutes. You may recall I didn't have a chance to finish showering. I'd like to do that sometime before the next millennium."

Gage's voice startled her. Mallory swung toward the door and then cried out at the movement. The door flew open. Gage charged into the small room. Mallory scooped up her shirt—his shirt—and covered herself. Only partly out of modesty—he'd already seen her unclothed—but more to hide the bruising. The last thing she wanted was to appear vulnerable to this man.

Anger warmed her cheeks. "Just what do you think you're doing?"

* * *

Eyes narrowed, Gage glanced around, looking for some threat. He found nothing and the tightness in his muscles eased. Until he looked to Mallory. His gaze sharpened on her. She was clutching his shirt to her front, but it didn't cover all of her. In the time since he'd last seen her, the swelling and bruising on her right side and back had worsened and were now deep and raw. He recalled how he'd slammed her onto her back when he'd taken her down in the bedroom. That had to have hurt. He couldn't say he'd never put bruises on a woman in the line of duty, and she'd sure as hell presented herself as hostile when she'd attacked him. He reminded himself that she'd been ready to put a hole in him with that glass shiv. Still, though he had cause, he regretted that he'd caused her additional hurt.

She was struggling to apply a damp washcloth to a nasty bruise between her shoulder blades. Gage frowned.

Mallory's eyes went hot. "If you've looked your fill, Broderick, you can close the door behind yourself."

Her insinuation that he was some sexual deviant getting his jollies peeping on her angered him. "Don't flatter yourself. You obviously can't reach that spot on your back. Give me the cloth." He reached out and gripped the washcloth.

"I can handle it. Now get out."

She jerked on his hold but he held on. At that slight jostling, she drew a sharp breath and paled. Gage released the washcloth at once.

He stuck his hands in the front pockets of his jeans. "Fine. Suit yourself."

She acted like he was some pervert. He left the room, but didn't go far, remaining outside the bathroom door. The woman looked about to keel over. The last thing he needed was for her to fall and break a bone.

Moments passed and she still didn't come out. He heard fumbling. Something hit the floor and she muttered under her breath, words he didn't catch. He gritted his teeth. This had gone on long enough.

"I said I want to shower," he called out. "Trying to treat yourself is holding me up. Now let me see to your injuries so we can both get on with our day."

She didn't reply, but when the bathroom door eased open, he took that as an invitation.

Back in the tiny room, she pierced him with a look. "What's the rush to get in here? Have a pressing engagement?"

As he was about to come back with a biting remark of his own, his attention was caught by her injuries. On closer inspection, he saw that her bruising was raw, livid, and extensive. She'd said Considine hadn't had time to interrogate her so this bruising was the result of something else. Out of necessity, Gage was now involved in her investigation. He didn't want to become any more involved in her business. But even as he told himself that, his mouth tightened and he had to ask. Had to know.

"How did you get these?" He pointed to the marks. "Husband? Boyfriend hurt you?"

Mallory drew back. "A lot of questions all of a sudden."

Ignoring that, he placed the cloth lightly on her back. She grimaced. She wasn't looking at him, had her head lowered, averted from him. Deliberately, he figured, so he wouldn't see her in pain. With her mind occupied by the discomfort, he didn't think she recalled the mirror in front of her that gave back her reflection.

She hadn't answered his question so he repeated it. "You got a husband who gets off hurting you?"

"I'm not married."

"Boyfriend, then?"

She shook her head, her lush brown hair sweeping gently across her shoulders. "Car accident."

Gage eased slightly at that. "You should have gone to a hospital." His exasperation was clear in his voice.

She gave him a level look. "You think? Thanks for that advice."

Gage felt his anger building at her sarcasm. His grip on the cloth clenched and he reminded himself to keep his touch light. "Well here's another unsolicited piece of advice. You're going to be sore for a while. I suggest you make use of a tube of ointment for muscle stiffness that's in the medicine cabinet." He tossed the washcloth in the sink. "Of course, it's your call."

Gage stepped away from her as she retrieved the cream from the medicine chest. He was about to leave her to it but stopped as she tried to spread ointment on a bruise in the center of her back that was beyond her reach. After a few seconds of watching her struggle, he scowled and held out his hand. "Let me do that."

Her face changed expression and he could see

she was searching for another option. He said nothing more, letting her work through it. He thought it a testament to how painful that bruise was that she gave in and handed him the tube.

Her hair was in the way. He gently pushed it aside. The silky smooth feel of the strands on his fingers had him pulling back as if he'd been burned. The sweep of hair fell across her back once again, but there was no way he was going to touch it a second time.

"Ah ... your hair ... " He held up a hand. "You need to move it so I can do this."

She wrapped her fingers around the mass and held it at her collarbone. Gage smeared cream on the bruise she'd been unable to reach, rubbing very gently. At his first touch, she drew a sharp breath but then released it and some of the tension in her body eased. He took that as an indicator that the cream had relieved some of the pain.

There was no bruising on her nape and upper shoulders but by her careful movements, he figured she had to be sore there as well. He applied cream and rubbed gently in slow circles. Again, she relaxed a little. He moved onto another spot on her back. Beneath his touch, her flesh warmed and her color heightened, taking on a rosy hue.

It was just skin, he told himself, as his throat worked. Her skin was not softer than that of any other woman he'd touched. Not smoother. The spray of freckles at her nape wasn't really shaped like a heart.

No, there was nothing more special about

Mallory Burke than any other woman. Problem was he just hadn't touched another woman since coming to the cabin. It wasn't this woman he was reacting to, he'd react to Godzilla's twin as long as she was female.

His hand was trembling and his breath had become more rapid. Despite what he'd been telling himself, his body wasn't buying it. He couldn't keep this up much longer. Already, he was as hard as granite.

He finished applying the cream quickly, then plopped the tube on the counter. "All done." He beat a hasty retreat.

Back in the kitchen, Gage braced both hands on the plain brown counter. What the hell had he been thinking, touching her? He must be out of his mind. Touching her had left him hard and ... twitchy. It had been all he could do not to take her in his arms and find out if she was agreeable to doing something about easing his state of arousal.

Not going to happen. He shook his head. Not going to happen. The wind screamed. The storm was showing no sign of ending. Goddamn it. He needed to get Mallory Burke the hell away from him.

* * *

Mallory heard him moving around in the cabin. After he'd tended to her, he'd fled as if she had a contagious disease. Of the two of them, hers had been the greater hardship. She thinned her lips. Clearly he hadn't enjoyed touching her.

She certainly hadn't enjoyed having him touch her either. It was necessary, and that was the reason she'd agreed. She was glad that was over and that he had no reason to put his hands on her again.

The cream felt good on her skin. Gage's touch had been so gentle. Surprising that hands that large could be so gentle. No doubt about it, the man had good hands.

Mallory frowned. She swallowed. What she meant was, he had a gentle and easy touch. Soothing. Comforting. Like a good masseuse. She cleared her suddenly dry throat. That was *all* she'd meant.

She put the shirt back on, helped herself to the aspirin, then went to the kitchen to get another bottle of water to wash down the pills. Gage was at the refrigerator, standing in front of the open door.

Their gazes met and he scowled again. She was here uninvited. She got that. But really, his constant reminders of that grated on her nerves.

"Bathroom's all yours," she said with some bite.

"Do I need to take the truck key into the shower with me?"

She gave him a wide eyed stare. "Why, is it dirty?"

With a pointed glare at her, he dug the key out of a front pocket of his jeans and replaced it on the hook. Mallory rolled her eyes.

He turned back to the fridge. As he reached inside, Mallory did as well. Their hands met briefly. She jerked her hand back. Gage did the same. She swung away from the refrigerator as he did and they collided. Her injured leg gave out and she fell back. Gage reached out, seizing her arms and keeping her on her feet.

His hold was tight and she could feel the warmth of his hands through the sweatshirt. She felt an awareness of him that she couldn't explain and didn't like. It left her uneasy. The cabin now seemed a lot smaller than it had an instant ago. Ridiculous. Crazy.

"I'm okay." Her words came out as a shout.

He released her at once, yet his touch seemed to linger. Silly thought. But she rubbed her arms up and down where his hands had been.

* * *

The throbbing in Gage's lower body had become full-fledged pulsing. He gritted his teeth. "Until the storm ends and I can get you off this mountain, I'm stuck with you."

"And I'm stuck with you," she countered.

He eyed her. "We're in pretty tight here. Let's stay out of each other's way."

She gave him a brisk nod. "Fine with me. We'll just have to make the best of it."

Gage turned away from her. Without glancing back he muttered, "There is no best of it."

* * *

He had a fascination with Don Corleone and had adopted the title of "Don" for himself, a title that commanded respect and instilled fear.

When he arrived at Billy Wilder's cabin, the Don didn't wait for his driver to open the door to the upscale SUV, but opened it himself and left the vehicle. The inclement weather would have prevented him from getting here at all if this cabin had not been low on the mountain and near the main road. As it was, the storm had severely extended the time to drive here and impatience was riding him hard. He moved as quickly as possible over the snow and ice to the front door.

Inside, the minions who worked for his minion Billy Wilder scurried out of his way or risked being mowed down as the Don made his way to the den where he told Wilder to await his arrival. The Don paid them no mind. His thoughts were consumed by the fact that his organization had been infiltrated by a federal agent.

One of the underlings sprang forward and flung open the door to the den. Wilder was seated behind a desk. His striped tie was askew. His thinning hair was disheveled as if he'd been running his fingers through it. An odor of perspiration carried on the air. Fear sweat. Wilder should be anxious and afraid. The Don pressed his lips together. It was Wilder's fault that they were in this situation now with the woman. The Don pinned Wilder with a look that had the man's Adam's apple bouncing.

Wilder sprang up from behind the desk and vacated the chair. "Hello, sir." His voice cracked.

Without returning the greeting, the Don commandeered the chair and said sharply,

"Where are they? I expected they would already be here."

Wilder's Adam's apple bobbed again. "On the way, sir. They should be here any minute."

Someone tapped lightly on the door on the heels of Wilder's statement. Without looking at him, the Don said, "That better be them."

Wilder admitted two men into the room. A woman was not with them.

"What are you two doing here?" Wilder said. "Get out." He flung out his arm. "Can't you see we're in the middle of something here?"

One man, a small, thin fellow coughed behind his hand. "As to that, if the something you're in the middle of has to do with Miles and Hugo, they aren't coming."

Wilder's face went corpse-pale. He cast a nervous glance to the Don. "What are you talking about?"

The small man spoke up again. "There was an accident. On the road. Miles and Hugo are dead."

"Wha—"

The Don could not have cared less about this Miles and Hugo. He cut off Wilder's sputtering. "And the woman? Is she also dead?"

If so, he would not be able to find out what she'd learned of his organization and who she'd told about it. He clenched his fist. Added to that, he would not have the pleasure of making her very, very sorry for involving herself in his business dealings.

"Gone," the thin man replied.

The Don spread his palms on the desk and rose slowly out of the chair. "What do you mean, gone?"

The underling patted the back of his hand against his upper lip that was now glistening with perspiration. He cleared his throat. "When Jim, here," he jutted his thumb in the direction of the stoop-shouldered man beside him, "and me come upon the crash site, we saw her. She saw us and hightailed it into the mountains. We left the van and chased her on foot but the snow was just coming down too hard and we lost her in the storm."

"You lost her!" Wilder got in the face of the small man. "You shouldn't have bothered coming back here without her!" Wilder turned to the Don. "Sir, I apologize for my people's incompetence. It's inexcusable. I'll make sure these two are severely discip–"

"There is only one thing you are going to do. And you are going to do this immediately."

Wilder opened wide, hopeful eyes. "Yes, sir? Anything."

The Don eyed Wilder, giving the man a look that had made many lose control of their bodily functions. Wilder's breathing became short and audible. Perspiration began to trickle down his cheeks.

The Don's voice vibrated with anger. "Find her."

CHAPTER FOUR

Gage's last words—there is no best of it—angered Mallory all over again. She had every intention of staying as far away from him as the tight space in the cabin allowed. With his disposition, he need not be concerned that she would be seeking out his company.

She went to the front door, giving the knob a twist. She hadn't locked it when she came inside with Gage's ID tight in her fist. She'd been distracted and angry. The door, though, was locked. He must have done that when she'd gone into the washroom for pain reliever.

Up here in this isolated location and in a blizzard, Gage had no reason to keep the door locked. Whether it was out of habit or training, she was glad to find it that way. Though, she acknowledged, the flimsy lock would not be a deterrent to Considine's crew.

"Thinking of going out again?" Gage said dryly.

She hadn't heard him come up behind her.

She faced him. "Checking the lock." She matched his tone, adding. "Not much of one."

"Don't need much of one. Just enough to keep the raccoons from turning the door knob and getting in on summer nights."

Summer nights? "When did you come up here?"

"August."

With that he left her and went into the bedroom.

It was now February. That made it ... six months.

If he'd been up here for six months, he wasn't on vacation. Could he also be working? That would explain his curt dismissal of her when she'd asked what he was doing up here. Being up here in the mountains could be a cover.

She followed him into the bedroom, stepping carefully to avoid the broken glass from the mirror that glittered on the floor. Gage had left her bra and panties, now dry, on the bed. He was at the chest of drawers, rifling through the contents.

Mallory went to him. "Are you working a case?"

He looked up from the drawer. "Do I look like I'm on the job?"

"That's not an answer."

"No, I'm not working."

"Is that the truth? Because I have no desire to mess up your case. I'm only asking because I need to know if we can also expect trouble from whatever you're involved in."

"No one's coming looking for me."

While she found that reassuring, she found it only marginally so. There was a finality to the words, to his tone, that she found unsettling. "When are you expected back at police headquarters?"

"What is this, twenty questions?"

"I want to know who I'm sharing space with."

He closed the drawer with a loud thud. "You're sharing my space, remember?"

Before she could press him further, he scooped up the clothing, walked by her and went into the hall. A couple of minutes later, she heard the shower.

Another non answer from her reluctant host. She was so ready to leave here. Leave him. But she did get the answer she needed. He wasn't working so she didn't have the added worry of someone he was involved with also showing up here.

Was there any chance the storm had ended during her conversation with Gage? In the living area she took up a position at the window. Leaning a hip on the wide sill, she pushed the curtains back with a fingertip. Of course the storm had not ended. Snow was coming down so hard it was impossible to make out individual flakes. It looked like solid sheets. The snow storm had likely saved her life, but at the moment she couldn't be thankful for the bad weather. As long as she was stuck here, she could do nothing for the women. Feeling helpless, she gripped the edge of the thick blue curtain in a tight fist.

Watching the storm would not make it stop and she would only drive herself crazy. She could feel her muscles tensed, ready to spring and her nerves as taut as bow strings.

She pushed off the window sill, letting the curtain fall back into place, then took the broom and dust pan from the kitchen and cleared the glass she'd broken in the bedroom. After, she put on her underthings.

She began a slow walk around the cabin. She needed to keep moving. She didn't want her muscles to stiffen any more than they had already or she feared she wouldn't be able to move at all.

Though there wasn't much ground to cover, she went only a few steps before she sagged into an armchair that matched the couch. So much for moving around. Each step was an adventure in pain and took her breath.

The bed things were still strewn across the couch. Clearly Broderick wasn't a stickler for neatness. He'd spent six months here. Six months. How often did he leave the mountain and go into town? Considering his unfriendly manner with her, she doubted he drove into town daily to socialize. A small chest freezer backed against one wall. If he'd stacked it with frozen meals, he'd have enough to last him for weeks or months at a time.

He had no means of communication. She couldn't imagine being out of touch with the world and the people she knew and loved.

She couldn't understand why he would choose this solitude. And over his job with the police department. Had the stress of the job gotten to him? Was he a disgraced cop who fled from a dishonorable conduct? Could he have been involved in something that provoked his leave from the Washington PD?

She wasn't comfortable with him. Part of that was due to his hostile reception. He'd made it clear that he didn't want her there, but that wasn't all of it. She didn't trust him. She knew next to nothing about him. The fact that he was not forthcoming, about anything, had her guard up around him.

A glance around the cabin showed very little that she could say for sure belonged to Gage. In the months he'd been here he hadn't accumulated much stuff. Aside from his outerwear by the door, there was just a set of weights and a bench press in one corner that she believed were his because the equipment looked well-used and would explain the hard muscled body she'd seen earlier and felt pressed against her. She didn't care for the thought and continued her inventory of the cabin.

A bookcase held an assortment of classics and hard boiled mysteries from the forties. There was a film of dust on the cases and spines. They hadn't been touched in a long time. Likely, the books belonged to the cabin's owner.

There were no photographs of Gage with people in his life. No souvenirs. No mementos. There was essentially nothing to give her a handle on the man, himself.

She heard the bathroom door open, then Gage emerged from the shower, dressed in fresh jeans and a T-shirt. The first word that popped into her mind to describe him was formidable. Another quickly followed, handsome as her mind filled with the image of his upper body without the shirt. The man was hot.

She blew out a breath. How he looked didn't matter to her. What did matter was the manner of man he was. She didn't have an adjective for that. She twisted her lips. Not a flattering one, at any rate.

Well, that wasn't exactly true. Despite his complaints about her being there—and they had been numerous—he had taken her in and treated her injuries. Treated them gently and with care which she had to admit surprised her, given his downright rude attitude.

The shower hadn't improved that attitude, she observed. The rest of the day went by without them exchanging a word and the silence continued as they ate chicken dinners. When Mallory was finished with her meal and had discarded the remains and washed her utensils, she went to the window. She pulled back the curtain just enough to see outside. It was still light out and the snow was still blowing strong.

"Tell me about Considine."

Gage's voice startled her after so many hours of silence, even if the question didn't. It was understandable that Considine would be on Gage's mind as well. Mallory released the curtain and turned to address Gage. Where to begin? "We've been wanting to go after Considine for a long time. Congressman Pritchard Manning spearheaded a task force dedicated to bringing down Considine. Considine's organization controls the drug trafficking, prostitution, and racketeering for the entire state. You name it."

She lifted a shoulder, let it fall. "We know all this, but haven't been able to touch him. On paper, he's as clean as that fresh snow outside."

"You said that the club you worked at is a front for human trafficking?"

"Yeah. That's a new one on Considine. We had no idea about that."

"Who owns the club?"

"It's registered to a William Wilder who is also the club manager," Mallory said. "I'm looking to tie him to Considine when we bust the trafficking operation open."

"What makes you think Considine is behind this trade?"

"From what I learned, the business is too big for him not to be. No way a small timer like Wilder is running that. For one thing, he doesn't have the brains. He's taking orders from someone. Considine is the logical choice. It has to be him!"

She could not keep how she felt about Considine in check and heard her own vehemence. As did Gage. His gaze grew intent on her.

"Right now," she went on, "my main concern is getting to the women before they're shipped out of the country. Once they're gone," Mallory shook her head slowly, "they'll be lost forever."

"Do you have a date for their transport?"

"No. Just their current location. Or, that is, their location as of when my cover was blown. Two men from the Don's crew were taking me to a cabin somewhere in these mountains to be interrogated when the car went off the road. That was the car accident I mentioned earlier. The men in the vehicle with me were killed but two more of Considine's people showed up and I had to make a run for it into the mountain. I lost them and ended up here. By now the women could have been moved." She rubbed her forehead where a headache was brewing between her brows. "I'm hoping that since Considine wanted to interrogate me, he doesn't know just what I found out about his organization. He may not know that I found out about the women."

"It's possible."

She heard the doubt in Gage's voice. "But you don't believe that."

"He might not take the chance and move them anyway."

She couldn't discount the possibility and it filled her with fear again for the women and desperation to be off this mountain.

A wave of dizziness had her grabbing for the wall to keep from falling face-first onto the floor. Eyes closed, she bowed her head to get a blood rush and stop the spinning.

"What's wrong?"

Mallory opened her eyes at the sound of Gage's voice, surprised to find him standing beside her. She was still holding the wall, but for some reason couldn't keep her body upright.

Gage put an arm around her. "Easy."

She didn't want to lean into him, but couldn't keep from doing so. His hold tightened and he swung her up into his arms.

As they moved away from the wall, she said, "I need—"

"What you need is to be horizontal for a while." He set her down gently on the couch. His brows lowered and he placed a hand to her forehead. "Shit. You're hot."

"No. No, I can't be sick."

"Looks like your body didn't get that memo. There's a thermometer in the first aid kit I used to clean your head wound. I'll be right back. Stay put."

The room had started another slow spin. She closed her eyes. In what felt like a second later, he was back. She opened her eyes that now felt as heavy as lead weights. Gage was watching her intently, deep creases of worry lining his brow.

He held up a thermometer. "Open."

She did as he asked and he inserted the thermometer into her mouth. When a beep sounded, indicating the temperature had been determined, Gage tugged the thermometer free. As he read the number, the creases between his brow deepened further.

He left her again briefly, returning with the aspirin and a bottle of water. Mallory raised her head and tried to do the same with her body, but fell back against the cushions. Gage wrapped an arm around her and raised her gently, taking her weight. He shook a few tablets into her palm then set the rest on the table and brought the water to her lips. When she'd swallowed the pills, he eased her back onto the couch.

She ground her head back and forth on the pillow. "I can't lay here. I need to keep watch for Considine." She made to rise off the couch.

"I'll keep watch," Gage said.

* * *

Gage placed a hand on Mallory's shoulder to keep her from rising and hurting herself, but she stopped trying to get up. Her eyes, bright with fever, closed. Another shudder shook her and she huddled into herself. He covered her with the blanket he'd used the night before, tucking it gently around her, but her trembling continued. Her face was pale but for two spots of red on her cheeks from the fever. He had no idea what was causing her temperature to rise. Had nothing here to find that out or to treat her with if he did determine a cause. He hoped to hell the aspirin would be enough to bring down the fever.

One thing he could do to help with that was to cool her off. He left her briefly, returning with a damp cloth that he softly passed along her cheeks then placed on her forehead. The cloth warmed quickly and he repeated the process. She'd said she was in a car accident. Did she have an internal injury? Would fever result from something like that? He didn't know. With the blizzard in full force, it would be some time before he could get her to a hospital. In the meantime, he hoped to find out that all this was nothing more than her body fighting off a cold.

Tremors rocked her. When he checked her temperature next, it had risen.

She curled into a tight ball. "How—high?"

"Another degree."

"It's rising fa-st."

"Yeah." He was silent a moment, not liking

what he knew he had to say next. "We need to break the fever. The aspirin and cloth on your brow aren't doing it. We need to wet you down."

She winced, then nodded.

"Do you need help with your clothes?" Gage said.

"I can man-age."

He left her to it and went to fill a basin with cool water, but when he returned, she'd lowered the blanket to her waist and lay fumbling with the shirt. He set the basin on the coffee table and gently removed her top. She was weak. Her arms were all but limp as he slid them from the sleeves. The fever was sapping her strength.

Tossing off the blanket completely, he took off the pants and socks, but left on her bra and panties. A concession to them both.

She was shuddering, her teeth chattering and though he wouldn't have thought it possible, she shrank into herself further. Seeing that, knowing he was about to cause her what would amount to pain, he hesitated. In the end though he was going to do this. Her body temperature had to be brought down. He had no choice.

He passed a hand down his face. "I'm going to turn you onto your stomach." He lifted her. She was trembling in his arms. Hell, she was burning up.

He set her back down on the couch carefully, facing him. Her eyes were closed. He sat beside her, dipped the cloth he'd been using on her forehead into the water and passed it across one shoulder. Gooseflesh pebbled her skin at once. She gasped and her back bowed. When her body dropped back to the sofa, she was still. Gage's heart rate jumped, but she was breathing. He closed his eyes briefly as his heart regulated, then continued on his course.

He continued to run the cloth over her until her skin cooled then gently turned her onto her back and did the same to the front of her body. He repeated the process again and again. The wind was howling now and flinging snow at the window and the walls of the cabin with audible thuds. The bit of light from outside that showed along the edges of the curtains faded. Gage left Mallory to douse the lights but for a small lamp on one end table then resumed his task.

He was still at it when the first weak streaks of dawn appeared. Mallory's lips moved and she mumbled something he didn't catch. It was the first sound she'd made in hours and he felt relief hearing it.

She now felt cool to the touch. A check with the thermometer showed that her fever was down. He brought the blanket to her shoulders, then rubbed a hand over his eyes and down his jaw. The night's growth of beard made a rasping sound.

Now that Mallory's condition had improved, he was beginning to feel the night without sleep. He'd been running on adrenaline. The rush ended and he was crashing. He couldn't let that happen. She was better but her fever could spike again. He couldn't take for granted that because her fever was down at the moment, it would remain so.

He plopped the cloth into the basin then went

into the kitchen, straight to the coffee pot which still had yesterday's coffee in it. It was as thick as sludge and bitter. Regardless, he drank deeply then poured a second cup and leaning back on the counter, stood watching Mallory, alert for any sudden movement.

The next moments brought no change with her or with conditions outside. The storm that had been raging since yesterday wasn't letting up. The day promised to be a dark one. Dawn had come and gone but it still looked like morning was breaking.

Gage finished his coffee, abandoned the mug on the counter and returned to Mallory. He placed his palm gently on her forehead. Still cool. When he straightened away from her, he found that she was watching him. She looked heavy-eyed from sleep. Her dark hair was tousled. Her lips fuller and a deeper shade of pink.

It was a combination that sent a punch of lust shooting through him. He felt a burst of self-directed disgust. The woman was ill. Still, he had to clear his throat before he could speak. "Morning."

"It's morning?"

"Has been for a while now."

The sleepy look was gone from her eyes in an instant, replaced by full-on panic. "What's happening outside?"

"No change." She visibly eased at that. "How do you feel?"

"Could I have another couple of aspirin?"

Gage lifted her so she could sit. He gave her two tablets and a bottle of water. "You should eat something. How about some soup?"

She swallowed the pills. "You can make soup?"

"I can heat soup. From a can."

She smiled. It was the first time he'd seen her smile. She had a crooked incisor and for some reason he found that small flaw wildly attractive. He felt an influx of blood where he needed it least. He steered his thoughts back to where they belonged: Soup.

He was still holding her to ensure she didn't slide down the couch. "Can you sit up alone while I get on that soup?"

"Yes."

He removed his arm from around her slowly and saw that she was able to maintain that position without his help. He went to the kitchen and began opening cupboards.

Mitch kept some stock items. Cans of soup among them. Gage found the double row of stacked cans on a top shelf. Chicken Noodle. Vegetable. Steak and Potato. He opted for the chicken noodle and fifteen minutes later carried a steaming bowl to her.

She was still seated as he'd left her, in the center of the couch but when she reached out for the bowl, he saw that her hands were unsteady. "Gonna need some help with that."

"I think I'll be fine on my own if this were in a mug."

He complied and while she sipped from a mug with a bison decal on it, Gage drank more coffee and kept an eye on her in case she faltered with the soup. Before she was half done, she leaned forward to set the mug on the table. He took the mug from her. "That's it?"

She nodded. Her eyelids drooped.

Gage watched her. "Get some more sleep."

She rubbed her eyes. "You haven't slept at all. You need to sleep. I'll be fine."

"I can manage one night without sleep."

She looked to him now. The strain was back in her eyes and it got to him. He was glad when her eyes drifted closed and he could no longer see it.

* * *

Mallory opened her eyes. Where was she? Her heart pounding, she realized she was still at the cabin. Considine hadn't found her.

How long had she been out? Was it still day or now night? Was it still snowing?

She heard the shrill cry of the wind and heard snow pelting the cabin. But those weren't the only sounds. She heard others, dull repetitive thuds, these inside the cabin.

With an effort she raised her head above the arm of the couch. Gage was stretched out on the bench press, lifting a barbell. As she watched, he blew out a breath, lowered the bar, lifted, then lowered it again.

He'd been at it a while by the look of him. Long enough to work up a sweat. Damp spots showed on the blue T-shirt he wore. Sweat sprang on his brow now as his biceps bulged with the strain and his chest swelled. Mallory's mouth went dry in a way that had nothing to do with the effects of the fever.

He paused, locking the barbell in position

above his head and his gaze honed on her like a laser. "You okay?"

"Fine." She gave a small shake of her head. "What time is it?"

"Ten."

"AM or PM?"

"AM."

She'd slept through a day.

Gage released a gust of air, then set the bar back on the brace with a clang of metal on metal and slid off the bench. A towel was draped over the back of the arm chair. He picked it up and swiped it across his brow. "How you feeling?"

"Better."

He crossed the short distance to her, pressed his palm to her brow. "Cool, but I want to take another look at your head wound anyway. Make sure it's not infected."

She could see the first aid kit on the kitchen table. He left her to retrieve it and make a stop at the fridge for juice and a sport drink. He poured juice into a glass then put the other bottle to his lips and drank deeply. When he'd all but drained it, he washed his hands, took the glass of juice from the counter, and snagged the kit.

He placed the items he carried on the coffee table. Standing over her, he gently parted her hair. Despite his light touch, Mallory grimaced. "How does it look?"

Gage smoothed back the hair that had fallen across her face. "Clean." He held out the glass of juice and more aspirin. "I need to shower. Will you be all right for a few minutes?"

"Fine. I'm fine."

He hesitated, peering at her from beneath brows that were now drawn together. He rubbed the back of his neck. "I won't be long."

She wanted to shower as well, but before she could, she'd need to be sure her legs would support her. She pressed her lips together in frustration, hating the weakness. "Take your time."

Though they believed an attack from Considine would come under cover of night, before he left her, Gage placed his gun on the sofa beside her.

True to his words, he was back with her quickly. He went into the kitchen and shortly after, the microwave began to hum. A few moments later, Gage set one of the two frozen meals he'd heated on the coffee table in front of her. Mallory's stomach balked at the thought of anything more than soup and when she voiced that, he brought her another mug of the chicken noodle.

The wind had increased. Instead of losing strength, apparently the storm was gaining. Even if the drapes hadn't been drawn, she wouldn't be able to make out the trees through the swirling snow, but this mountain had been rich in them. "Must be pretty here when there isn't a storm happening."

"I never noticed."

She hadn't realized she'd spoken aloud until he'd responded. She frowned at his comment. He'd spent six months in these mountains, how could he not have noticed their beauty? She would have asked him about that, but since he wasn't big on conversation, she kept the thought to herself.

Once he'd delivered her soup, he'd returned to the counter to eat his meal as he had before. He said nothing more now. She wondered if he was naturally a man of few words or if the solitude had made him so. Or, maybe the reason he wasn't chatty was a night and most of a morning without sleep. "Why don't you go into the bedroom and get some sleep?"

"I can go without a little longer."

She gave a little hum of agreement. "A hazard from pulling all nighters on the job—or a perk, some would say."

"In my case, it's a result of all the coffee I drank."

Mallory winced. "I don't know if what I saw in your cup earlier could still be considered coffee."

"Point taken. I never did get around to making a fresh pot."

"You might want to get on that. That stuff you were drinking looked like battery acid."

He gave a little laugh. "Tasted like it could be."

He had faint lines at the side of his mouth that suggested he'd done a lot of laughing in his life, that being unfriendly and unapproachable weren't the norm for him. Mallory wondered what was.

Gage pushed off the counter and went to her. "You're looking a little flushed." He reached out and touched her forehead. "Still cool."

"Glad to hear that." Her relief was evident in her tone. She didn't want to repeat the night she'd just had.

Gage gave a little grunt in what sounded like relief as well. "Let's keep up the aspirin for today anyway. Okay?"

"Yes. If the fever comes back, next step I think will be a cold bath. I'd rather avoid that."

"A cold bath will cause chills which would end up increasing your body temperature. Would have to be lukewarm. Regardless, I'd also prefer we didn't have to put you through that. I found a bottle of ibuprofen in the back of the cupboard under the bathroom sink. If we need to, we can alternate with the aspirin. They have different elements that will work on bringing down your fever."

Mallory's brows arched in surprise. "Where did you learn so much about this?"

Gage's eye lids lowered, shielding his gaze. His eyes became shuttered as she'd seen them do once before. Something she'd said? Surely not. They'd been talking about treating fever. What then? She opened her mouth to ask if he was all right, but before she could he spoke.

"Focus on getting well." His voice was hard. "When the snow lets up, I don't want to have to delay getting you off this mountain."

He left her and went into the bedroom, slamming the door.

CHAPTER FIVE

Gage had retreated to the bedroom to get the sleep he needed, Mallory presumed. Despite his unprovoked outburst, he returned to her three hours later to check her temperature. She'd told him that wasn't necessary, that she was monitoring herself. He'd made no comment at all and three hours after that was back again to stick the thermometer in her mouth.

He was just as closed-off as he had been immediately following his outburst. Clearly he wasn't a man who got over a bout of temper quickly.

She'd been on the verge of rethinking Gage Broderick. For an instant, she'd thought she'd glimpsed another side of him. A lighter side. Her mistake, obviously, and now that she thought about it, it was well and good that she'd been mistaken. That lighter side had been attractive. She was already physically attracted to him. The last thing she needed was to actually like him and deepen that attraction. Well, she need not be concerned about that.

On one of his temperature checks, he'd taken time to brew coffee and while he was on watch, she'd taken that time to shower and to change into one of Gage's warm T-shirts that covered her to her knees.

That was hours ago. Now, Mallory huddled more deeply into the blanket, clutching the ends so hard her fingers cramped. She was freezing and not from fever. The temperature inside had dropped drastically. The cabin felt as cold as a meat locker.

The bedroom door opened. Gage wasn't due to check on her for some time yet. The cold must have awakened him. The lights were off in the cabin. She only saw him emerge because of the long-barreled flashlight he held that gave off a wide beam of light.

He hadn't changed for bed and was still dressed as he had been in a T-shirt and jeans. He cast a quick glance her way but didn't acknowledge her, and didn't break pace, continuing on to the window.

So he was still in a mood. Her lips firmed. She would have been content to just leave him to it, but at the moment that wasn't an option. "What's going on with the heat?" Her tone was as frosty as the temperature in the cabin.

"Generator tank must have emptied."

Of course, that would explain the cold. Another thought struck her that had her insides quivering. She leaned forward on the couch. "On its own? Could someone have emptied it?"

"It's a possibility."

Mallory's stomach clenched. "You're not going out there to check are you?"

He peered briefly into the darkness, then let the curtain fall and turned to her. He shook his head. "Gas could have been emptied in an attempt to get me outside." His jaw tightened. "Someone may be looking to take me out so he can get to you."

Mallory shivered as much from his words as the cold.

He crossed the room then returned to her, his parka in hand. "Put this on. I'll get a fire going."

"Should we do that? We might give ourselves away."

"No way of knowing when the storm will end. If we don't, we could freeze by that time and then it won't matter. And if someone has tampered with the generator, they already know we're in here so there's no reason to be discreet."

He crouched by the fireplace and took wood from the crate. He struck a match, and brought it to several pieces of kindling. As the flames caught, one by one he tossed each strip of wood into the fire.

Mallory shivered. She left the couch and moved close to the flames. Gage added more wood, a few thick logs that looked like they'd burn for hours.

"We're going to need to stay close to the fire if we're going to stay warm," Gage said. He went into the bedroom, dragged the mattress in front of the fireplace, then took several blankets and comforters from the linen closet and added them to what was already on the bed. "All yours."

Mallory lowered herself onto the mattress and got beneath the mound of covers Gage had provided. For himself, Gage moved the armchair from the living room and brought it to the hearth. He put on the other parka then took a seat.

A silence ensued in which only the wind and the pop and hiss of the logs in the fire could be heard. For her part, Mallory couldn't have made conversation if she'd wanted to. Though Gage had placed the mattress as close to the fire as possible, she was still freezing. Her teeth chattered nonstop and her body trembled from the cold.

Gage rose from the chair with a creak of leather and then his shadow fell across Mallory. "We need to get you warm."

He joined her on the mattress, setting his gun down within easy reach. He lifted the blankets briefly while he got under them with her, then lay on his side and put his arms around her.

Mallory hesitated, battling with awkwardness at being pressed up against a man she hardly knew. It was ridiculous to feel embarrassed after she'd been so exposed to him while he'd tended to her injuries and treated her illness, yet she did. But the delicious heat he offered overrode her embarrassment. Meeting his gaze, she nodded and leaned into him. He hadn't fastened his jacket and now wrapped that around her as well.

She was snug in his arms. Her cheek rested against his hard chest. Though they were both fully clothed and also wore overcoats, their position was unquestionably intimate. Pressed tight as they were, light couldn't pass between them and when her gaze traveled upward, she saw each individual whisker that darkened his strong jaw.

She lowered her gaze not liking that her eyes had wandered. Well, okay, what else was she supposed to look at? Gage filled her range of vision. Or so she told herself. But even as she did, she sacrificed some of the blessed heat, and turned so her back was now against Gage's front and he was out of her view.

* * *

Mallory turned in his arms. Gage bit down on his molars to stifle a groan as her sweet ass pressed against his groin. He needed to put some distance between their lower bodies and end the torment. End some of it. As long as he held her pressed to him, with her scent filling his every breath, there was no way his body would be at ease. Hell, at this point, though, he'd take anything he could get. He shifted position, introducing a few precious inches of space between them and closed his eyes, willing his body back under control.

The woman had a man after her intent on killing her. Her would-be assassin might have someone outside now, waiting for a chance to get to her. That's what Gage needed to keep his mind on. That was *all* he needed to be thinking of when it came to her.

He let out a long breath. "You need to get some sleep." She was still recovering from the car accident and from a bout of fever and, maybe if she were asleep, he'd no longer think of sinking his body into hers.

"Hard to sleep with Considine possibly outside waiting to make a move," Mallory said.

She spoke in a whisper. The strain in her voice cut through his thoughts of sex. Her body was stiff in his arms, her muscles pulled taut. He was holding her tight and now relaxed his grip just enough that he could turn her gently so she was no longer facing the door, but faced him. Her cheeks were pale. Her eyes were heavy and red rimmed from fatigue. She was fighting off the sleep she so clearly needed.

"We're ready if they make a move." Gage didn't add, with their meager arsenal. "We don't know that Considine has tracked you yet. We're looking to be gone before he does."

"I'm for that."

"I want to remind you that we're not going to be able to drive my truck down the mountain. The roads this high up don't get plowed. Once the storm ends and we can see past the end of our noses out there, we're going to need to make our way out of here on foot."

"Yes, of course," Mallory said quietly

"When we get down the mountain, we'll be able to drive from there. Mitch had an old truck when he bought this place. Truck's parked at the bottom of the mountain. We'll use it to drive you to the nearest cop shop. You can contact the Bureau from there."

"Mitch left the key to the truck?"

"Yeah. It's by the fridge, on the same ring as

the cabin key." Gage studied her a moment. "You've been sick and you have a bum foot. You need to get as much rest as you can before we leave here."

"I'll be fine." She swallowed. "I have to be. This isn't just about me—about us, Gage." Her voice throbbed with emotion. "I have to get back and relay the information about the women."

"Don't take this on yourself," he said gently. "Don't make yourself responsible for the outcome."

Mallory's features pulled taut and her cheeks reddened with temper. "Maybe that's the kind of cop you are, Broderick. Abandoning your command for six months to come up here."

His jaw tightened and his own temper sparked at her words but he couldn't sustain it, not when she was right. That was exactly the kind of cop he now was. That was exactly what he'd done.

Mallory squeezed her eyes tight for an instant. When she opened them, she focused on Gage. "I'm sorry. That was uncalled for. You're right about not taking this onto myself, but I can't do that. Not with this investigation."

There was pain in her voice and in her eyes and Gage found he wasn't immune to it. He reached up and brushed his thumb along her cheek. "It's hard to keep a distance."

"Is that what happened to you?" Her tone softened. "Why you're up here instead of in Washington?"

He removed his hand from her face. "No. Get some sleep. I'll keep watch."

Her gaze remained on his, her eyes probing.

After a moment, she broke eye contact and nodded. "Wake me in a couple of hours and I'll take over so you can get some rest as well."

* * *

Mallory opened her eyes. Gage was gently shaking her shoulder and saying her name. It must be her turn to keep watch. She'd slept badly, fitfully, but she had slept.

She pushed hair back from her face. "I'm awake." Her voice was thick from sleep. She cleared her throat. "Your turn."

"Not that. Storm's over."

Mallory held her breath. No screeching wind. No thuds from snow striking the cabin. Gage moved away from her and went into the kitchen. Mallory lumbered to her feet and made her way to the window. She parted the drapes a few inches. Moonlight streamed in.

Gage spoke from behind her. "Before we leave, I'm going to take a look outside. Make sure we don't have company."

Mallory wanted them to be on their way as much as she wanted her next breath, yet she hesitated. "I don't like you going out there. You could be walking into an ambush. It'll be daylight in a couple hours. We'll be able to see this whole area then and if anyone is out there."

"We can't blow this chance."

His implication was they may not get another one if they waited. "Okay then, I'll go with you. Or instead of you." This was her investigation, after all.

"Your leg will slow you down in that snow. If there's trouble, you'll need to get out of there fast."

Then he was gone. She went to the window. She caught sight of him briefly under the full moon, then he stepped into the shadow of the trees and blended into the darkness.

With the absence of the wind, all was still outside and there was a preternatural quiet that she found terrifying. Her heart pounded like a jackhammer. Surely if Gage had encountered someone, there would be some movement, some sound.

The cabin door opened and Gage stood in the doorway. "We're clear. Time to go."

He wrapped gauze around Mallory's injured ankle, then wound tape tightly around it several times. When he was done, Mallory tested the support and nodded.

While she put on the parka's hood and the gloves, Gage pocketed the keys to Mitchell Turner's truck and doused the fire. They left the cabin with Gage in the lead. Though he'd deemed the area clear, his gun was gripped in his gloved hand.

On the porch, Gage paused and glanced around. Mallory did the same. The absence of sound struck her. She found the silence eerie and unsettling. Her nerves, already frayed, vibrated like tuning forks.

Gage glanced back at her and nodded, then took her hand and they made their way down the steps and into the snow.

The contrast to their surroundings from the

last two days was startling. Moonlight struck the snow and it glittered. A scent of pine came off the trees and carried on the air. The view looked post card pretty. The view, coupled with the stillness and quiet made the setting appear serene. It was a false sense of calm, Mallory thought, with the bombs they'd planted among the trees.

The sounds of several engines cut the silence. High-pitched whines These vehicles were coming at them from beyond the trees, and approaching fast.

Gage slid an arm around her waist, and half carried her, seeking shelter behind a tall Evergreen. Headlights cut through the darkness then two snowmobiles broke through the trees.

One of the snowmobiles drove into one of Gage's traps and the driver was pulled from the vehicle. The man landed in a bloody heap in the snow and that snowmobile, now out of control, spun and struck a tree.

The second driver must have spotted them. He turned the vehicle in their direction, headed straight for them. He raised a gun and an instant later, a bullet clipped one of the branches inches above Gage's head.

"Get down!" Gage shouted to be heard above the roar of the engine.

His hand landed on Mallory's head and he pushed her to her knees behind him. Gage brought his gun up, took aim and fired. The man cried out and clutched his chest. An instant later the snowmobile spun, dislodging the driver, and barreled into a snow bank.

Gage didn't waste a moment. He clutched

Mallory's hand again and they were off, moving toward the snowmobile. Gage backed the vehicle out of the snow. Mallory climbed on behind him, and put her arms around his waist.

Three more snowmobiles came out of the trees. Gage gunned the engine. Using one hand to steer and maintain their speed, he raised the gun and took aim.

Their vehicle fishtailed. The mark was lost and Gage cursed. In those few seconds, the snowmobiles following them gained more ground.

"Give me the gun!" Mallory shouted. "You can't aim and drive!"

Seconds later she saw that he could. Gage took aim again, then fired into the trees, igniting one of the home made bombs. A boom, and then flames erupted. He fired again with the same result. One of the snowmobiles, in the path of the fire, swerved and collided head-on with a second vehicle.

The third emerged from the billowing smoke as Gage reached the mountain road. Mallory glanced back at their pursuer. The snowmobile continued to glide over the snow, coming at them now at top speed.

A bullet shattered one of the side mirrors, spraying glass.

Again, Gage shouted, "Get down!"

Mallory noticed he was watching his rear view through the one remaining mirror carefully. He reduced speed.

"Gage! What are you doing?"

He didn't respond. Their pursuer fell back,

zigzagging over the snow behind them, and coming up beside them. As Mallory watched, the driver raised his gun. "Gage! Look out!"

But he didn't need the warning, she realized. He was tracking the other snowmobile. His arm was already up, the gun aimed. He fired. Blood spurted from the man's neck. The snowmobile veered out of control and overturned.

Gage swung to face Mallory. "You okay?" When she didn't answer immediately, his tone sharpened. "Mallory?"

"Yes." She released a pent-up breath. "By the way, good shooting."

He kept his eyes on her for another instant, then glanced at their rear view again. "I don't see anyone else on our tail. That may have been the last of them for now."

The "for now" had Mallory taking another look behind them. "How much farther to Turner's truck?"

"We're almost there."

They descended the rest of the mountain without incident. The pickup truck was an early model behemoth that had seen better days. Gage got the vehicle started and with a bounce that lifted Mallory off the seat, they left the mountain behind.

She braced her hand on the dashboard. "How far is the town from here?"

"I don't think we should take you into town. I don't want to risk you being spotted. Your office is in Bradley, right?" At her nod he continued. "We're about three hours out. Safer to take you there. Until we hit the interstate, stay below the windows."

Thirty minutes later he steered the truck onto the highway. "Okay, we're clear."

Mallory sat and buckled up. Her stomach growled.

Gage glanced at her. "There's a rest stop coming up, but I'd rather forego it and get you to the Bureau."

"I agree. My stomach can wait. I want to get to the office as soon as possible."

The interstate had been cleared of snow. She focused on the traffic outside her window, willing them to reach the Bureau office quickly. The old truck's heater provided little warmth. She was glad of Gage's parka and huddled into it.

They drove without speaking for the most part but the drive was far from quiet. The wind whistled. The engine hummed and traffic whooshed as it sped by.

Gage, she was sure, had more on his mind than idle banter. His features were strained and his body was tense. Several times, she'd observed him checking the view behind them or glancing in her direction. Clearly, he was alert should another threat present itself.

When they entered the small city of Bradley, Mallory gave Gage directions to the Bureau office. He pulled to a stop in front of the door to the building.

Mallory removed her seat belt. "York, my boss, will want to speak with you too."

"I expected that. I'll park and meet you inside."

In the small building, she led Gage to the office

of Special Agent in Charge Jeffrey York. York was a sturdy man, built like a bull with close cropped gray hair and a trim moustache. Mallory made the introductions and the men shook hands. York listened intently as Mallory updated him on the situation, then Gage added details of his own.

Mallory shifted in the seat. She wanted to get to the warehouse and it was taking a force of will for her to sit through this briefing

When Gage finished speaking, York picked up the phone and punched numbers. "I'm getting a team together to go into that warehouse."

Mallory leaned forward on the chair. "I want to be part of that team."

York nodded. "We'll meet in the briefing room." He turned to Gage. "Appreciate your help on this Captain Broderick. If you could wait here, I'd like to speak with you again."

Gage agreed.

With all that had happened, Mallory hadn't had a chance to contemplate saying goodbye, but Gage's agreement brought on a release of tension and, for some reason, a profound relief.

In the briefing room, the team leader laid out strategy for the strike. Mallory dressed in her gear and joined the other agents in a truck. Nerves were riding her hard. The lives of twelve women depended on everything going right.

They arrived at the warehouse a short time later. The proximity of it, to the city, to the Bureau office struck her, along with Considine's audacity to keep these women so close with no fear of detection.

All was quiet outside the warehouse. Though

Mallory was straining to get inside, she recognized the team leader's prudence in observing the scene before proceeding. When more time passed without movement, the leader gave the signal to "Go".

Mallory took up her assigned position by the door. On another signal from the leader, she entered the warehouse.

The building was dark and cold. Her breath puffed out with each exhalation. The women would need heat if they were to survive. Considine would not be careless with what he considered his merchandise and her stomach churned with the fear they were too late and the women were no longer here.

Weapon drawn, she moved deeper into the warehouse. A rodent scurried out of her path.

She turned a corner and came to a door. Flattening herself against the wall, she put her gloved hand on the knob and yanked the door open. Her fear was confirmed. The room was empty.

The team leader came up behind her. "We've finished checking out the rest of the place, Burke. Empty and clean. There's nothing to suggest anyone was here. We're packing it in."

* * *

Once Mallory went with the team to converge on the warehouse, York had asked Gage to go over what had taken place at the cabin again. After, Gage had declined York's offer to wait in his office for Mallory's return and had opted to wait in the hall. A door opened. Gage wheeled toward it. A redhead, heels tapping a staccato beat, crossed the tile and entered one of the offices. Gage rolled his shoulders to relieve a knot of tension there, but it remained. Another door opened. But it was only a man pushing a mail cart.

Gage needed to call Mitch and let him know what went down at the cabin. The thought flitted through his mind but was dismissed as he focused once again on the exit door.

He was pacing the length of the hallway when the rumble of the elevators at the far end drew his attention. He spun toward them. A soft ding heralded the opening of the double doors. A tall man in combat gear stepped out and after him—Mallory.

Without blinking, Gage marked her passage down the hall until she entered York's office. He rolled his shoulders and this time felt a release of the tension.

A phone was on a table in the reception area, along with a scattering of magazines. He dropped onto one of the padded chairs and called Mitch.

Two rings later, Mitch came on the line. "Mitch," Gage said.

"Hey. Where you calling from?"

"Bradley."

"I caught a weather report out your way. Hell of a day for a drive."

"Yeah. Mitch, I'm calling to let you know that you can expect to hear from the PD out here." Mitch was also a cop. They'd met when they'd both been at the academy. Twelve years later, they were still tight. Mitch was now police chief of a district. Gage told him what went down at the cabin.

Mitch's voice tensed. "You okay?"

"Yeah. Fine."

"What's the status of the investigation? How deeply are you involved?"

"Investigation is ongoing. Now that Agent Burke is back at the Bureau office, my part in this is done. I'll be driving back up to the cabin later today."

Mitch was quiet for a beat. "I was hoping you were going to say you had enough of the place."

Gage didn't have an answer for that, so he said nothing.

"I was hoping you were going to tell me you're going back to the job," Mitch added quietly.

No, Gage couldn't do that. He wasn't fit to command. He didn't expect he ever would be again.

When again, Gage offered no response, Mitch said, "If you need anything."

"Just the cabin."

"It's yours for as long as you want it, you know that."

"Appreciate it."

"Gage—"

"I gotta go. Give my love to Shelby." Shelby was Mitch's fiancée.

"She worries about you, you know."

Though Gage did know that Shelby worried about him, that was Mitch's way of saying he worried.

"Take care of yourself," Mitch said.

"You, too."

* * *

While the rest of the team changed out of their gear, Mallory accompanied the team leader to York's office. Inside, the leader updated their superior on what had gone down at the warehouse.

"... and there's nothing there to show that the women were ever there." The team leader concluded. "Sorry, Burke."

Mallory acknowledged the sympathy with a nod.

York pressed his lips together. "Then there certainly isn't anything to show us where they might have been moved."

"No."

After the team leader left, Mallory remained in York's office. "Sir, we need to get Billy Wilder, the owner of the club, in here and sweat him. He abducted a federal agent. To save himself, he'll give up the location of the women and then his boss, Considine."

York drummed his fingers on his desk. "I'm already on it. Our people are on the way to round him up. I'll call you when we have him."

"I'd like to be in on the interrogation."

York nodded. "You've earned that. I'll be in touch. For now, go home."

Mallory left York's office. She found Gage in the reception area.

"The women?" he said.

She shook her head. "Considine moved them."

Gage cursed under his breath.

"Yeah," she agreed.

"You okay?"

"Far from it," Mallory said. "Not only were the women moved, but it looks like they were never there. "York's having Billy picked up in connection with my abduction."

"Once Wilder is in custody, the Bureau will have a shot at Considine. From what you've told me, the first real shot. You know Wilder. Is he likely to flip on his boss?"

She sneered. "Wilder will talk. He'll have no choice. Once he's picked up, Considine will mark him and Billy's hours will be numbered. Billy knows that. He'll be terrified to turn against Considine, but he'll realize that we're his only chance to stay alive."

"Things will happen fast then once Wilder is apprehended."

"Can't happen fast enough for me." She tapped her leg in a gesture of impatience. "York said he'd call when Wilder's in custody. Nothing more I can do here."

"I'll drive you home."

CHAPTER SIX

Gage hadn't planned on remaining with Mallory after he drove her to the Bureau office. As he'd told Mitch on the phone, he'd planned to turn right around and drive back up to the cabin today. If York hadn't had a chance to explain the situation at the cabin to local law enforcement, Gage imagined the sheriff's office would have questions for him.

But then he'd learned from Mallory that the women had not been found and that Billy Wilder was still at large. As long as he was, Mallory was still a target. Her fight, as important as it was, wasn't his. He'd lost his fight six months ago. But the thought of Mallory in danger had his gut clenching and he hadn't been able to walk away.

"Can we make a stop on the way to my place?"

Mallory's voice pulled him from his thoughts. "Sure. We should take you to a hospital. Have you checked out. I doubt you told York about the car accident or your injured ankle so he wouldn't stop you from going on that raid."

"You're right. I didn't mention any of that to York. There's a clinic not far from my place. We'll make a stop there, but I need to go somewhere else first."

Gage narrowed his eyes at her urgent tone. "Where?"

"It's silly. Beyond silly, but I want to go back to the warehouse. I want to take one more look inside."

"You think something might have been overlooked?"

"No. Maybe. I said it's silly, but it's something I need to do."

He saw it was gnawing at her. "Which way?"

She gave him directions and shortly after, he parked the truck in front of the warehouse. It was situated at the end of a dirt road with no other buildings on it. Anyone traveling on this road would be destined for the warehouse.

Any trace of the FBI raid a couple of hours earlier was gone and the building appeared deserted. His truck was the only vehicle on the lot.

Still, appearances could deceive and according to Mallory's information, until recently, this warehouse had been used in the commission of a crime. Until he knew for sure that Considine's people hadn't returned, Gage wasn't taking any chances. When Mallory opened her door, he put a hand on her arm and detained her. "Someone may have come back here since you and the team cleared out. Did you get your service weapon replaced?"

"Yes."

"Keep it handy."

Mallory took her gun from her purse and Gage saw the purse now also held a new cell phone. Along with his own weapon, Gage added a police-issue flashlight from the glove box and they left the truck.

The air outside was cold but inside, the warehouse was only slightly warmer than out. The day was overcast with low hanging clouds and only scant light filtered in through the pair of windows set high in the walls. A panel on one wall held the circuit breakers that would turn on the lights. Gage saw no harm in lighting the place. Even if anyone did arrive, his truck parked outside would give notice that someone was at the warehouse. But when he flicked one of the breakers up, no light came on.

Mallory glanced up at the unlit florescents in the ceiling. "No heat. No lights, either."

Gage flicked on the flashlight. "Who is the warehouse registered to? Obviously not Wilder or anyone that could be traced back to Considine."

"York will check it out, but it's likely linked to some dummy corporation in some part of the world that no one has ever heard of."

Mallory took the lead and Gage followed her to the back of the warehouse. Outside light decreased as they went deeper, but enough light remained for them to see where they were walking. Mallory's steps were sure-footed with purpose. She came to a thick steel door. It opened into a twelve by twelve cell with concrete walls and floors. This room, cut off from all sunlight, was dark as a grave and just as cold.

"This is where I think they were being kept." Mallory's voice echoed.

She wrapped her arms around herself in a tight hug. Gage didn't believe it was the cold she was attempting to stave off since she still wore her combat gear with insulation that would keep more than the cold from reaching her.

She took a turn around the room. "Can you shine some light in here?"

Gage swept the beam in a slow arc.

Mallory's eyes followed the path of the light. "I was all over this place—this room— with the team." Her voice lowered as she took herself back. "I don't know what I was expecting to accomplish by coming here again. What I expected to find that might give us a clue to where they were taken. Maybe I was expecting that they would be here hidden somewhere." She shook her head. "I've seen enough, Gage. I'm ready to go."

"Maybe it was just simply a matter of you needing to do something rather than sitting around waiting for something to happen."

She looked up at him. "Thanks for not calling me crazy."

"You care. Nothing crazy about that."

Though the depth of her interest went beyond that of a job. At the cabin, Gage had noted that she was vested in the outcome.

Gage drove next to the Bradley Clinic. After Mallory spoke with the secretary and filled out the necessary forms, they took seats in the waiting room.

She checked her cell phone for messages. "A

bunch. None from York. Most from my brother, John."

While Mallory called her brother, Gage got up to stretch his legs. He returned as she ended the call and resumed his seat beside her.

Mallory returned the phone to her purse. "John's been trying to get in touch with me for weeks."

She grew pensive. Gage reached over and tipped up her chin so he could look into her eyes. "Everything okay?"

"Yeah. John and I try not to go too long without contact but with his job and my job, it's not always possible to stay in regular touch."

Her brother was obviously important to her. "Your brother also with the Bureau?"

"CIA."

"You sound worried."

"I always worry. Just as I know he worries about me. But it's what he does. What we do. We both live with that." She chuckled. "He told me he's met someone. Wants me to meet her the first chance we get. Sounds serious."

"Why is that funny?"

"It's hard to picture my brother in love. Sometimes John can be, well, like you." Her eyes twinkled. "Stubborn. Grumpy. Set in his ways."

Gage scowled. "Whoa. Stop. My ego can't take all this praise."

Mallory's name was called. As she got to her feet, she glanced back at Gage and grinned. "Remind me where I left off with that list. There's more."

"Can't wait to hear it." Gage's dry tone

prompted another laugh from her.

The doctor found nothing more damaging in Mallory than an assortment of bruises, abrasions, and a sprained ankle, all at various stages of healing. As Gage drove them away from the clinic, she called York. Her conversation was brief. Agents had gone to Wilder's residence and his place of business. He wasn't at either location. York had issued a nation wide alert to law enforcement.

When her conversation with York ended, Mallory sat clutching her phone. Frustration was coming off her in waves. "Billy's holed up somewhere. By now he may be out of the country. We may never find him." She made a sound of disgust. "York has the search warrants. He's sending a team over to the club. I want to meet them."

* * *

They grabbed a quick takeout meal and ate as Gage drove to The Wild Club.

He dropped a food wrapper into the now empty take out bag. "I'll do a drive-by first in case anyone other than your team is there."

In the seat beside him, Mallory surveyed their surroundings. No cars were on the lot and no lights were on inside. Only the marquee with a gyrating figure of a woman glowed against the night sky. "The place looks abandoned."

"Yeah." Gage parked across the street from the club. "We'll wait here for your team to arrive."

"Shouldn't be too long." Mallory's voice

trailed off and she squinted into the darkness. "Did you see that? A light went on for an instant. On the main floor."

"Yeah, I did. This place have a silent alarm?"

"No. Billy, and more Considine, wouldn't want police coming in here." Her heart rate accelerated. "Maybe it's Billy in there. I can't wait for the team to get here, Gage. I have to check this out."

He picked up the flashlight. "Let's go."

The air was cold. Mallory hunched deeper into her jacket. The side door of the club was unlocked. They drew their weapons. She exchanged a nod with Gage and they went inside.

Streetlights and the blinking light from the marquee lit their path. Mallory knew the layout and the location of furniture and other items. The light they'd seen had come from somewhere down here. They worked their way through the main floor. Nothing was disturbed and no one else was there.

"Billy's office is upstairs," Mallory whispered.

She led Gage to the back of the club and they took the stairs to the second floor. Wilder's office door was open. Moonlight filtered in through the slats of a dusty blind. Desk. Filing cabinet. A photo copier. An assortment of potted plants on a stand. They checked the storage room and a restroom, completing their search of this floor. Here as well, nothing appeared out of place and they were alone.

Mallory lowered her gun. "If Billy was here, he's gone." She used the phone on Billy's desk to call York and update him on the events that had led to her and Gage entering the club, and to advise York that she was on site. York ended the call to coordinate a canvass of the perimeter around the club with local law enforcement.

Papers lay across the desk. She fingered a couple. One was an invoice from a dry cleaner for table linens. The second was an estimate for a furnace replacement.

Mallory opened a desk drawer. The odor of cheap men's cologne wafted into the air. She recognized it as Wilder's usual scent.

Gage winced. "What the hell?"

"Wilder's aftershave."

Along with the cologne, there was an assortment of business cards strewn in the drawer. Suppliers of liquor, food, and linens. The cards were not arranged either alphabetically or by service. Organized, Wilder was not.

She opened another drawer and found a fifth of Scotch with half the bottle empty and a crystal tumbler. She was itching to start the search, but anything obtained in an illegal search and seizure would be inadmissable in court. If she went ahead prematurely, Billy and Considine could walk away on a technicality. Disgusted, she closed the drawer.

Gage went still. "Do you smell that?"

"All I can smell is Billy's cologne." But as she said that, another unmistakable odor overrode the nauseatingly sweet scent and Mallory's breath caught. "Smoke."

Gage was already across the room. He yanked his shirt from his jeans and wrapped the tails around his hand, then seized the door knob and gave it a twist. The hall was filled with smoke. With Mallory in pursuit, he went to the top of the stairs they'd just climbed. Flames were visible at the foot of the steps.

"Smell that?" Gage pitched his voice to be heard above the roar of the flames.

"Gasoline. Someone started this."

"Yeah. No getting out of here the way we came in."

They returned to Billy's office and went to the window.

Gage's hand fisted on the sill. "A sheer drop."

"There's a fire escape on the roof," Mallory said. "The stairwell is at the end of this hall."

Gage went into the small adjoining bathroom and spent a couple of precious minutes soaking two thick cotton towels. He handed one to her. She didn't need to ask what to do with it and held it over her nose and mouth.

She fell into step with Gage but in her haste, twisted her weak ankle. Gage reached back for her, preventing her from falling but she struck the plant stand and the brightly painted clay pots toppled and crashed against the tile. A key lay in the dirt. Mallory grabbed it.

Gage clutched her hand. "Let's go."

Smoke had risen and now filled the corridor. It was difficult to see through the dense fog. Gage moved to the wall with her in tow, leaned a shoulder against it, and using the wall as a guide began to make his way down the hallway. The heat was intense. Perspiration coated her skin. Her hand grew slick in Gage's.

Despite the thick towel, smoke penetrated and

Mallory began to cough. Gage looked to her in concern and she nodded to reassure him.

Flames now rose behind them. The railing was engulfed and collapsed. Sparks flew into the air. Gage's arm swept around her shoulders and he brought her against his chest, shielding her with his body as they continued down the hall. After what seemed like an interminable walk, they reached the door to the stairwell.

Gage removed the towel from his face and wrapped it around his hand, feeling for a door knob. When he found it he opened the door, holding it for her to precede him.

With the door closed, the roar of the fire was silenced and the stairwell became as dark as night. They turned on their flashlights and began the ascent to the roof, their steps echoing in the stairwell. After climbing several stairs, Mallory's step faltered and Gage wrapped an arm around her waist, taking weight off her healing leg.

When they reached the top, he opened the door. They coughed as they took their first breath of fresh air. The moonlight showed his face, black with soot. His eyes were red and streaming. She must have been in the same condition because he passed the towel gently over her face, then did the same for himself.

At the fire escape, he slung the towel around his neck. "I'll climb down first in case your leg gives out."

All was quiet as they made their descent. She'd expected to hear sirens from fire trucks responding to the blaze, but as of yet, there were none. It had seemed like so much time had passed since they made their way from Wilder's office, but only minutes had gone by.

Through the breaks in the steel stairs, Mallory saw an alley below. As they neared the bottom, the odor of garbage carried on the breeze from an overflowing Dumpster. Two cats hissed and shrieked over some bit of refuse.

In the alley, Gage lifted her off the stairs and set her on the ground. Gun in hand, he peered at the road beyond, lit by street lamps. "We need to keep our eyes open for whoever started the fire. He may still be lurking, wanting to make sure the job was complete."

After a few tense seconds, they left the alley. They were no longer in front of the club. The alley led to a road made up of row housing.

Gage took her hand once again and steered her out of the glow cast by the streetlights. "I don't like the coincidence of the club being torched when you were there. We know the fire was deliberate. You may not have been the target, but until we've ruled that out, I'm going to presume that you were."

A wail of police sirens and a bleat of horns from a fire truck broke the quiet. Someone had reported the fire.

"You think we were followed here?" Mallory said.

Gage slowed his pace to match her shorter stride. "Either that or someone knew you were going to be here tonight. From what you've told me, Considine's reach is far. He may have been informed about the search planned tonight and figured a fire would be a good way to get rid of anything incriminating at the club and take you out. I don't want to go back to your apartment tonight. Considine may have the place staked out. I think we should spend the night somewhere off the grid."

"If Considine is watching, he would have made the truck. Better not to go back to it either." Mallory tugged Gage's hand. "This way." She took the first turn they came to, leading Gage onto another street made up of seedy bars and clubs. "There's a motel about a block over. No one will expect us to go there."

Again, they kept to the shadows, though there was no one else on this street. They reached the motel illuminated by a flashing neon sign.

Gage released her hand. "Wait here while I check us in. No reason the clerk has to see you."

He opened the door to the registration office and before he closed it behind himself, Mallory glimpsed a man on a ladder back chair, his chin on his chest, dozing. A television sat on a shelf behind the man, tuned to a black and white movie.

Gage registered quickly and joined her outside. He was holding a paper bag.

Mallory pointed to it. "What's that?"

"The clerk told me that the motel doesn't provide any toiletries. I figured we're going to need some."

Mallory glanced at her sooty hands. "Good call."

Gage stopped on a cracked asphalt path. "We're in room thirty one." He looked around. "That way."

103

The old motel wasn't equipped with key cards. Gage let them into their room with an old bronze key. Intermittent light from a flashing neon sign in front of the motel provided glimpses of the interior. Mallory made out a double bed in the center of the room with a nightstand on each side. A television sat on an old metal stand at the foot of the bed.

Gage went to the window, pulled the curtains closed then thumbed the light switch. The bulb in the ceiling, in a plain white shade, flickered then lit.

The decor left much to be desired with the color scheme predominantly bright oranges and lime greens. On closer inspection, the furniture looked like it had been purchased during the nineteen seventies.

Much to Mallory's surprise, the place was clean and she detected a faint trace of some bleach-based cleaning product.

Gage picked up the TV remote. "Go ahead and shower first. I want to see if the fire has made the local news yet."

Mallory wanted to know that herself and went to stand beside him. He channel surfed for a couple of minutes, then stopped at a scene of a female reporter backlit by a burning building.

Mallory leaned a little closer to the television. "There it is."

"Fire fighters are battling this blaze which broke out at Twenty-Four Stowe Street, a popular bar that features exotic dancing," the reporter said. "The club is closed for the night and it's believed the building is unoccupied. At this time, it is not known what started the fire. A full investigation is expected. Now, back to you Nancy at the news desk."

Gage flicked to another news station. The same footage was repeated.

Mallory picked up the phone on the nightstand and called York to let him know she'd made it out of the fire and to find out if he'd had any word about Billy. Gage turned away from the television and focused on her. At York's "no', Mallory shook her head at Gage. The conversation with York ended after that.

She replaced the phone in the cradle. "I'm off to take that shower."

Twenty minutes later, she'd made liberal use of the products Gage had purchased. The motel didn't supply a bathrobe and putting on her filthy clothing that reeked of smoke again was unthinkable. Mallory took one of the white towels and wrapped it around herself, knotting it at her breasts. The towel fell only to mid-thigh. As far as modesty went, it left much to be desired.

When she joined Gage in the bedroom, she saw just how immodest reflected in his eyes. His deep blues fixed on her and went darker, before he caught himself and looked away.

In that instant, before he'd banked it, a flame lit in his eyes. Desire, pure and simple. Seeing it sparked a heat inside her as well.

Her breath caught and it took her an instant to regain control over it so she could speak. "Shower's yours. You might want to wait a few minutes for more hot water."

"Not a problem."

He breezed by her and into the bathroom.

* * *

In the privacy of the small washroom, Gage rubbed a hand down his face that was not steady. Hot water? Hell, no. The last thing he needed was to get any hotter.

When Mallory had joined him in the bedroom wearing nothing but that towel he'd all but swallowed his tongue.

She'd washed her clothes and hung them on the towel bar. Among her jeans and blouse were her bra and panties. Saliva pooled in his mouth. He recalled all too vividly the sexy body that wore those items.

He turned away from her underthings and to the shower. He twisted the taps then stepped beneath the pulsing water. An image of Mallory in here with him, water sluicing down her naked body came to him, and then him following the path of the flowing water with his mouth. He reached out and gave the tap for the cold water another hard twist.

He finished showering. He pushed his wet hair back from his face then reached for a towel to wrap around his hips. Among his purchases from the clerk, was a razor. Gage rubbed the stubble on his jaw. To hell with it.

Back in the bedroom, Mallory was seated on the bed, against the head board. Her hair had dried some and now tendrils of the thick brown strands framed her face softly and curled around her bare shoulders. Seated as she was, her breasts strained against the towel and Gage got rock hard again.

He looked away from her and to the television in an effort to distract himself. But the dresser was against the wall behind the TV, with its large mirror, and Mallory was reflected in all her splendor in the looking glass.

"Are you going to stand there all night?"

Gage turned to her. "What?"

"Guess we should have asked for a cot, though I'd be surprised if this place had them."

"No problem." Gage cleared his throat. "I'll sleep on the floor."

"The floor is hard and cold. This bed is large enough. No reason we shouldn't both get a good night's sleep."

Sleep? With her in bed with him? Good luck. He'd already tried that and failed and now that he knew what it was like to have her in his bed, his mind went to work supplying him with memories of her pressed tight to him. He blew out a breath. Oh, yeah, no sleep for him tonight.

* * *

The mattress dipped as Gage got into the bed with her. Mallory recalled what that solid body had felt like against her own when they'd shared the mattress at the cabin. A slow burn began in her lower belly and was spreading. Maybe sharing a bed hadn't been her best idea. But she certainly didn't want him to have to spend the night on the floor because she couldn't reign in her hormones. She was just going to have to make the best of it.

He placed the gun on the nightstand then stretched out on his back giving her a view of his chest and abs. The muscles there were well defined and her gaze lingered. He hadn't shaved and the stubble on his cheeks and jaw only made him look sexier.

"Do you mind if I turn out the light?" If she couldn't see him, she'd be able to put him out of her mind. She hoped.

"Go ahead."

She left the bed and turned off the ceiling light but left the bathroom light on with the door slightly ajar so they could find their way around the unfamiliar surroundings.

In that couple of minutes out of the bed, she got cold. She shivered and burrowed beneath the blanket. "Good night."

"Night."

His voice sounded strained. "Are you getting a cold?"

"No. Good night."

She turned on her side and pulled the blanket up to her nose.

* * *

The temperature in the room dropped as the night got colder. In her sleep, Mallory had been inching across the bed. When her body touched Gage's, he broke into a sweat.

He wanted to shift away from her. The feel of her against him was driving him out of his mind, but she was shivering from the cold. He put his arms around her. As his body heat penetrated she relaxed, grew warm and soft against him.

Her scent had been teasing him all night. She'd washed with the same soap and shampoo he'd used, but on her the fragrance had become something else altogether. Something that could not be found in a cosmetics bottle. It was her. All her.

She shifted slightly and her hand slid across his abdomen. He groaned.

* * *

Mallory felt deliciously warm. Slowly she became aware that she was pressed tight to a hard, male body. Gage. Her head was on his chest. One of her legs was atop one of his and his arms were banded around her. He was still on his side of the bed. It was she who'd moved.

She looked up. In the light streaming in from the bathroom, she could see that his gaze was on her. Desire sparked in his eyes. Her heart pounded. With his gaze locked on her, he ran his thumb tenderly across her cheek. A thrill of anticipation surged through her. When he bent his head to hers, she was already moving to him.

A breath from her lips, he went still. His muscles tensed. He vaulted from the bed, taking her with him. She was about to ask him what had possibly distracted him when she heard it. A scrape in the door lock.

Gage grabbed her hand and the gun from the nightstand. He led her to the wall behind the door, and took up a position in front of her. He chambered a round in the gun then pulled the door open.

Early morning light filled the room and a man fell forward. Tall. Broad in the shoulders but sagging around the middle. He looked like an ex-jock going to fat. Gage hooked him around the neck and jammed the barrel of the gun into his temple.

The man uttered a small cry. Something dropped out of his hands and fell to the floor. It was a key. The guy lifted his arms, clawing at Gage in an attempt to break Gage's hold. It was a useless endeavor. Gage tightened his grip and put an end to the useless struggle.

Mallory stepped out from behind Gage. Her eyes lowered to the key. Gage was also looking at it. He hadn't missed the fact that it was a key rather than some crude instrument that was being used to get into their room, either. Was the man Gage had subdued one of Considine's men? Had Considine tracked them to this motel room and bribed or killed the clerk for the key?

Gage gave the man a shake that knocked his teeth together. "Who are you?"

"Oliver." The man cried out. "Joseph Oliver."

"Why were you breaking into this room?"

Oliver squealed. "Not breaking in."

Gage's muscles bunched as he increased his grip on the man's throat. His voice dropped to a lethal whisper. "If you want to walk out of here, start talking."

"It's the—the truth. I swear it. I mean no harm to you and to your—your lady." The man was stuttering and tears filled his eyes. "I made a mistake, that's all. Don't have my glasses. Wrong ro-om. I swear it!"

The man was now trembling in Gage's hold. As far as assassin's went, this one lacked the constitution for the job, Mallory thought. Was it possible he was telling the truth? Gage's eyes narrowed and Mallory believed he was wondering the same thing.

Gage gave the man another shake. "What's your room number?"

"Thirty seven. I forgot my glasses when I left my room. I thought this was my room. I'm sorry. I'm sorry."

Gage met Mallory's gaze. "Mind getting the key?"

She picked it up. "Thirty seven." Their room was thirty one. It was possible he'd mistaken the number.

"Where's your ID?" Gage said.

"My co- coat pocket."

Gage nodded to Mallory. She took out the man's wallet and found a driver's licence. "Joseph Oliver." She recited an address in Oregon. "What are you doing here, Joseph?"

"I'm attending a conference. I sell insurance."

She found a business card that confirmed his occupation.

Gage raised a brow. "Your company didn't spring for much in the way of accommodation."

The man licked his lips. "This isn't where I'm staying. I—ah—met a girl."

A white line showed on his ring finger where he'd worn a wedding band until recently. The man was an adulterer, Mallory thought with disgust, but not an assassin. After this experience, she'd be surprised if he stepped out on his wife again.

Gage released Oliver. The man's hands went to his throat, rubbing where Gage had no doubt hurt him. Mallory returned his key.

"Thank you. Thank you."

Gage eyed Oliver. "Get out."

Joseph Oliver ran.

The room was now as cold inside as out. Mallory hugged herself against the chill.

Gage closed the door. "I think we can leave here now."

"Think so."

Gage nodded. "We'd better get dressed then."

But she noticed his gaze went to the rumpled bed where they'd been about to make love and held. He passed a hand back through his hair and blew out a long breath before turning away.

She knew how he felt. She was all too aware of being in that bed with him as well.

CHAPTER SEVEN

Gage hadn't raised the subject of how close they came to making love in the motel room and Mallory hadn't either. Might have been better if they had. Might have cleared the air. Or, maybe they would have picked up where they'd left off. She wasn't sure how she felt about that. She was attracted to him. Her insides tightened now reminding her just how much.

She'd never been swept away by attraction as she was with him. Her cooler head had always prevailed. Maybe it had been for the best that this one time when her cool head had failed her, fate had intervened in the form of Joseph Oliver. She shifted position and cut off the thought that it didn't feel like the best.

When they'd left the motel, they didn't go back to the club for the truck, but left it to be towed and stored in impound. They took a cab to a car rental agency and picked out an inconspicious compact, then when they'd arrived at Mallory's apartment, they'd searched to make sure the place was unoccupied by anyone other than themselves.

Now they were eating scrambled eggs in Mallory's living room with the key they'd obtained from Billy's office on the coffee table in front of them.

They'd both taken showers and changed clothing. The clothes Gage had worn during the fire were spinning in her dryer and he'd changed into fresh clothes that her brother had left here on his last visit. Mallory's brother John and Gage were the same size and the clothes fit well, but Mallory had never noticed that John was as broad in the shoulders or as solid in the chest as Gage. She recalled what those shoulders and chest had felt like when Gage had held her in his arms. She reached for the cold glass of orange juice on the table and drank deeply to cool the fire that ignited within her.

Gage set his empty plate down. "I want to check out the key. Looks like it might fit a locker at a bus or train station. Either of those local?"

Mallory brought her focus back to the investigation. "Both."

He glanced at his watch. "How about it?"

Mallory nodded, and hoped that Billy had not rented a locker in another city.

The train station was closest to her apartment so they went there first. Inside, travelers toted bags and pulled luggage. A woman rocked a crying infant in her arms.

The young mother was in the center of the aisle and Mallory skirted her as she made her way to the banks of lockers at the back of the station. They were looking for locker one hundred eleven, according to the numbers on the key.

Gage took one end of the lockers. Mallory took the other. When she found a locker with the matching number, she signaled to Gage. He stuck the key in the lock.

"What are you doing there? That's my locker."

A man came up beside Gage. Forty something with shaggy hair tied back in a ponytail.

Gage recovered nicely. "My mistake."

They backed away and took up a position by the wall in full view of the locker. The man swung the door open, revealing an assortment of clothing on hangers, several pairs of shoes and a uniform that belonged to a cleaning store. He retrieved the uniform and headed in the direction of the rest rooms.

Mallory shook her head. "Nothing suspicious there."

Gage followed the man with his eyes. When the guy was out of sight, Gage returned to the locker. "To be sure." He stuck the key in once again and twisted. It didn't fit. "Onto the bus station."

Unlike the train station, there were few people about. Ticket sellers held conversations among themselves. A man was stretched out across several seats, asleep. The aromas of coffee and fresh cinnamon buns filled the air.

Mallory pointed the lockers out to Gage. They found the number they wanted and this time when Gage inserted the key, the door opened. Mallory reached inside and removed the single item, a sealed manilla envelope.

Gage closed the locker door. "Back to your place where we can check that out."

* * *

Mallory sank down on her couch and removed a thick sheaf of papers from the envelope.

There were several photographs of young women, each individual photo stapled to a page that listed vital statistics—height—weight—hair color—date of birth—health status. She read each in turn then passed them to Gage, seated beside her on the arm of the sofa.

He took his time studying the pages. "Looks like a full work up was done on each woman."

"And then some. Look at the writing on the back of the photos."

"2/15 p.m." He turned over another. "3/12 p.m."

Mallory tapped the photo she held. "The handwriting is definitely Wilder's. I saw his scribble enough times when I was working at the club to recognize it, but what do the notes mean? The numbers?"

"At a glance it looks like a notation of time. The dates the women were taken and that they were taken in the afternoons." Gage turned the other photos around. "The numbers vary but not the letters: p.m. Why would it be noted that the girls were taken in the afternoons? Doesn't make sense which leads me to believe the letters mean something else."

"Found some loose photos." Mallory flipped

through them. "These don't have any notations." She paused. "This photo is Cindy Mars. The woman I told you about who Wilder claimed came in for a job but was turned away because of her lack of talent."

Gage looked at the picture. "Wilder kept her around long enough to take a still."

Mallory picked up another paper. "Here's one with Billy's personal information. Bank account numbers. A deed to his cabin." She moved on and came to a listing of internet websites. She passed the pages to Gage.

While Gage bent over the papers, she left the table and went to the hall closet for her laptop. Back at the coffee table, she powered up, then keyed in one of the website addresses.

"Hmm. A dating site." She read the features. "There are several chat rooms." She tried a few of the other addresses. "These are dating sites as well. All with chat rooms." She stared at the laptop screen. "Do you think this is how they're doing it? How they're targeting the women?"

"Looks like it could be," Gage said. "This would work for the traffickers. Pictures and profiles are posted. All they have to do is make a selection, then establish contact."

"Billy stashed this info for a reason. Makes sense he'd want to keep this part of the business away from the club. To be conducted away from the club." Mallory paused, working through it. "No, I don't believe that. He was not running this operation. Too slick. Too sophisticated. Obviously he knew about it, but he was subordinate, taking orders from Considine. Could be he assembled this data as insurance."

"Wilder may have wanted some leverage against his 'Don' should he need it. Would come in handy if he got busted and needed to cut a deal with law enforcement."

"Maybe Wilder isn't as stupid as I thought." She tapped the keyboard. "I want to build a profile, Gage, based on the information on these papers from Wilder's locker. I'm going to post that profile to these sites on Billy's list."

"Going to need more than one if you don't want whoever's trolling these sites to make you as a plant."

He was right. "Several profiles then. We'll see who bites. I need to do this right. Make the descriptions irresistible to whoever is luring these women."

Mallory put on a pot of coffee for Gage and brewed tea for herself. She needed ideas and needed to think. When the beverages were ready, she poured cups for herself and Gage and returned to the living room with them.

She hunched over her laptop. "The women in Billy's photos are all brunettes. Between eighteen and twenty one." She selected nineteen as the age for her profile and added that to the physical description. "Now for variety, I'll play around with ethnicity and interests." After she was done, she turned the laptop toward Gage. "What do you think?"

He read the profiles carefully. "Nice job."

Mallory took a sip of her tea. Stone cold. She winced and set the cup back on the table. "Next for the photographs. Can't use mine since they know me." She opened a software program.

Night had fallen by the time they'd finished. Her apartment window showed stars and a view of the skyline. Mallory left the sofa to turn on lights then uploaded the profiles through a secure account at the Bureau so an IP address would not be traced back to her.

She leaned back against the couch. "I'm starved. I have some take out menus in the drawer by the stove." She left the sofa and returned with them. "What'll it be?"

They decided on pizza with the works from a mom and pop restaurant where Mallory often ate.

"While we're waiting, we can cross reference the loose photos with the Bureau's missing person's data base." She keyed in her password, then scanned the photos one by one. "Well, this is curious."

"What?"

"Only Cindy Mars is listed as missing."

Gage leaned over her shoulder for a look. "I don't know squat about hair styles and make-up, but I'd say those looks aren't current. How far back did you search?"

"I thought of those things too and went back ten years, well before any of these shots were taken. Still, no one was flagged."

Gage rubbed his index finger back and forth beneath his chin in thought. "Try something else. Upload those photos onto the internet. See if you get any matches."

Mallory did as Gage suggested. "Here's an obit for Molly Combs."

"Cause of death mentioned?"

Mallory scanned the entry. "... after a brief battle with cancer. We got an entry for Rita Castile. It's an advertisement for a club where she was listed as a dancer." Mallory clicked on the link. "The entry goes back six years."

"A long time in a dancer's life. Rita may have moved on."

"Yeah." Mallory's intercom buzzed. "That'll be Ernie from the restaurant."

A few minutes later, Mallory took the box from the gangly son of the restaurant owners. "Thanks, Ernie."

"No prob, Mallory."

She set out plates and a couple of bottles of beer. Again, they ate at the coffee table. Gage resumed his seat on the arm of the couch. Mallory sat cross-legged on the carpeting.

She bit into a slice of the pizza. "We got another hit. This one, Sherry Herron, is listed as a dancer here in Bradley. Since they're all dancers, I'm wondering if they have any connection to the trafficking operation at all or if Wilder just liked the way they looked and downloaded their photos for himself."

Gage reached into the pizza box. "Did Wilder bring in any new dancers that resemble these women in hair color or skin tone?"

"Not that I saw. You thinking these girls worked for Billy at some point?"

Gage folded his slice in half and brought it to his mouth. "It would be a connection. We won't know unless we ask them."

"Even if they did work for Billy, I don't see how that would tie in with the trafficking ring."

Mallory wiped her hands with a napkin. "I don't want to waste time going off in a direction that won't help us find the women."

Gage took another slice from the box. "I agree but we won't know if there's a connection if we don't look into it. Your call."

They had no leads. She wasn't in a position to discount anything. "One of the women is local. There's still time to see her tonight."

* * *

Gage pushed open the door to the Arctic Club. The air was thick with cigarette smoke and from a blue fog that floated off the stage as part of the current dancer's routine.

The patrons were three deep and he pushed his way through, making a path for himself and Mallory to the bar. Once there, he made space for Mallory to stand in front of him, then signaled the bartender and ordered two bottles of beer.

Rather than ask if Sherry Herron was working and risk alerting anyone of their interest, they took their drinks to one of the few empty tables and settled in. If Sherry was working, then eventually she'd appear on stage.

Gage scanned the crowd, but their entrance didn't appear to attract any attention. With Wilder still at large, Gage was concerned about Mallory being in a location he could not secure. When he'd voiced his concern to her, and told her he would follow up on this alone, he'd been shot down. So here they were. But he didn't like it. The fire at the club was still fresh in his mind.

He couldn't be casual about her safety. He kept his eyes trained on their surroundings.

They sat out three sets. The fog, the noise and the worry, had given Gage one hell of a headache. The music changed and another girl took center stage. The new woman was older than Billy's photograph of her, but there was no mistaking the petite brunette. It was Sherry Herron. Beside him, Mallory gave him a look.

Sherry had a long set, then with a wave and a smacking kiss goodbye to the audience, she left the stage.

Gage leaned over and spoke into Mallory's ear. "We should speak with her outside. Not in here."

Inside their rental, they watched the door to the parking lot. When Sherry emerged, she wasn't alone. Another of the dancers who'd performed earlier was with her.

"Better to catch Sherry alone," Mallory said.

Gage watched the women share a laugh as they linked arms and made their way over the patches of snow and ice. "I'll follow at a distance until she's dropped off the other woman or is dropped off somewhere herself."

Sherry was the driver. She got behind the wheel of a sporty red coop. They didn't have long to wait before she turned into an apartment complex and the other dancer got out of the passenger side.

Sherry drove on. A short while later, she pulled up to a modest house.

Gage parked the car. "You take the lead on this. A man approaching her in her driveway at this time of night might spook her."

Mallory left the car. Gage got out after her, but stood against the hood of the rental, remaining close by.

Mallory joined Sherry on the driveway. "Sherry."

The other woman swung around. Her hand, covered in a purple woolen glove, flew to her throat.

"Hello." Mallory stopped a few feet from the other woman. "I'm Agent Mallory Burke." Mallory held up her ID. "This is Captain Broderick. We'd like to speak with you."

"What's this about?" Sherry lowered her hand. "It's after midnight."

"We didn't want to interrupt you at the club."

"You were at the Arctic?"

"Yes." Mallory pocketed her ID. "We won't take up much of your time. Did you work at The Wild Club in town?"

Sherry huffed out a breath that fogged in the cold air. "Why are you asking me about that job? It was a long time ago."

Mallory tilted her head and gave the woman a penetrating stare. "How long ago?"

"I don't know. Three, four years, something like that."

"How long did you work there?"

"Six months, I think, give or take. Why is this important?"

Mallory ignored the question. "Why did you leave?"

Sherry's heavily painted lips pursed. "I don't see why I should tell you that. But if it will get rid of you faster, I left because I got a better offer at another club. More money, you know how it is. Listen, it's really late and I'm working tomorrow."

"Just another couple of questions, Sherry. Do you remember any of the other dancers who worked there when you did?"

"No. I was there to make a living, not to make friends. I didn't socialize with any of the other girls."

"What about Billy Wilder? Did you socialize with him?"

Sherry scoffed. "No way. I don't mess where I eat, got that? No way I was going to be in a position to get canned if the boss got tired of having me in his bed. Like I said, I was there to dance and that's all I did there. Now I'm done answering your questions." She jutted out her hip and braced a hand there. "If you got any more for me, you can ask them in front of a lawyer."

Sherry turned and went into the house.

* * *

Though he was too long for Mallory's couch with the armrest extending only to his calf, it wasn't the sofa's fault that Gage couldn't sleep. That he was alert to every sound in the apartment. The heat kicking on. The hum of the refrigerator. The ticking of the kitchen clock. Alert to Mallory, one room away.

He could smell her light perfume that wafted in the air and hear her moving on the mattress. Movement that was followed by a sharp intake of breath and a small groan of pain.

Gage tossed back the blanket. The door to the

little bathroom off her bedroom was ajar. She was standing, one hand braced on the soft blue counter, head lowered. He rapped on the door with one knuckle. Her head came up. "You okay?"

"My ankle's acting up. Since the fire. All that stair climbing, I guess."

Gage entered the room. "Let me take a look." With ease, he lifted her onto the counter, then took her foot gently in his hands. The ankle was swollen. "I'll get something cold to put on it."

She didn't have any bags of frozen vegetables in her freezer, he saw a couple of minutes later. He wrapped some ice cubes in a dish cloth then returned to her. He placed the ice on the swelling which also placed him in line with her breasts. She was wearing a white tank top over some purple pajama pants and when she leaned forward to look down at her ankle he got a glimpse of her sexy cleavage, minus a bra.

She released a sigh. "Feels good."

He was glad that her pain had eased, but he had a feeling his pain was about to climb to a new level. Along with her foot, the rest of her must also be getting cold from the ice. Her nipples were now pressing against the soft material of the top. His heart rate rose and he hardened.

* * *

Gage still wore his jeans but his torso was bare. Mallory didn't want to stare but found it impossible not to.

She could smell him. A trace of sweat. Heat.

Something grittier that hit her system like a drug. Her heart began to beat in what felt like triple time. A fire started inside her.

This time there was no Joseph Oliver. There was just herself and Gage.

She didn't need anything more on her mind now than the investigation. She'd only known Gage for a few days and knew so little about him.

And none of that mattered at this moment. She wanted this. Wanted him.

* * *

Gage closed his eyes and when he opened them, Mallory's gaze was on his. Her eyes had gone soft, liquid, and in that moment he was sure he'd never wanted anything more in his life than to be able to lose himself in them. To lose himself in her. To step outside of himself for a time. Leave the hurt and insanity of the last six months behind for a while, and engage in mindless sex where his body took over to give and to receive nothing but pleasure.

He rose to his feet. With their gazes still locked, Mallory spread her knees and he stepped between them. He wanted to touch her everywhere at once but for some reason started with her hand. He took it in his and pressed her palm to his lips.

"Gage," she murmured.

At the sound of his name on her lips, he pulled her to the edge of the counter so her lower body was now against his and kissed her as he'd been imagining for far too long.

Open-mouthed. Wet. Hot. Mallory wound her

arms around his neck and rocked forward, bringing his erection right against her center. Her action sent a blood rush to his arousal. Gage lifted her completely off the counter and into his arms. She wrapped her legs around him, keeping their bodies flush as he carried her to the bedroom.

Only the lamp on the nightstand was lit, but it was enough light for him to find his way. He tumbled with her onto the bed. Bracing over her, he raised the hem of her tank top. His body went white-hot as he caressed and kissed her breasts. Mallory moved restlessly against him, then reached out and unzipped his jeans. She found him, hot and pulsing and moved her fingers up and down in a caress sure to shatter whatever self-control he had left.

Before that happened, he slid down her body, taking her pajama bottoms and panties down with him. When he reached his destination, he parted her gently, and entered her with his tongue. His strokes were long and slow and unrelenting. Mallory let out a gasp of pleasure and then a groan that went on and on. Hearing her in pleasure ratcheted up his own and drove him closer to the edge.

Her body bowed and as she threw her head back, her hair fanned out on the crisp sheets patterned with tiny flowers. She began to writhe. Gage was trembling now, almost at the breaking point. Bracing himself over her, he eased into her. He squeezed his eyes shut and clenched his jaw at the power of the sensation of being inside her.

Mallory dug her nails into his biceps and wrapped her legs around his hips, taking him deeper. Gage hissed as she hit every nerve.

It had been too long for him and she was so incredible. So sweet. He had to caution himself to take it slow, not to let instinct and inclination take over and ram into her.

But Mallory made the decision for him. She arched her back, plunging him deeper and after that there was no going back for either of them.

Gage kissed her, tasting her lips, sucking her tongue into his mouth and began to move. Mallory matched his rhythm and then he was lost. He closed his eyes and uttered a groan with his release that blended with Mallory's soft cry and gasps as she reached her own climax.

CHAPTER EIGHT

Gage stayed with his face buried in her neck for a long moment. Only the thought that he was likely crushing her into the mattress could make him move at this point. With effort, he rolled off her and onto his back.

Mallory's eyes were closed. The back of her wrist lay across her brow. "I don't know how you were able to move. I'm too spent to open my eyes."

"It wasn't without great effort."

"I can believe that." She took a deep breath through her nose, let it out slowly in a long, drawn out sigh. Her lips curved slowly. "Wow, Broderick. I mean wow!"

"Right back at you, Burke."

"In a few minutes. Or a month. I'll see what I can find for us in the kitchen and we'll have a kind of picnic in here."

"A picnic?"

"Yeah," she said. "Sure. Just without the ants."

Gage found himself smiling at the notion.

A short while later, Mallory managed to rouse herself and return with food. Their picnic consisted of leftover pizza, a beer for Gage and a glass of wine for herself. The aroma of spicy pepperoni blended with the scents of beer and wine.

Gage rose onto an elbow to accept the beer she held out. Mallory's bedroom was decorated in blends of grays and purples. He snagged a vibrant lavender cushion and set it against the headboard, then leaned back. "Gotta hand it to you, you put together a mean picnic."

"Not so much tonight." She laughed, fully exposing that crooked tooth and he recalled running his tongue over it when he'd been exploring her mouth. "But I've been known to. I've had plenty of experience. My family was big on picnics." Gage tipped back the beer bottle and took a drink. "You live in New York, but I don't hear New York in your voice."

"Chicago." She picked up a pizza slice from the box and transferred it to one of the two plates she'd placed on the bed between them. "Born there and lived there until I went away to college in California."

Her thick hair was tousled from their lovemaking and he couldn't resist taking a lock between this fingers. "Bet you were hell on a surf board."

She rolled her eyes and took a healthy bite. "Hardly." She chewed, then took another chunk out of the slice. "I've never been on a surf board."

"Come on. There wasn't some surfer dude

wanting to teach you the sport?"

She laughed again. "Nope. Actually, I was a book worm in college. Didn't know any surfer dudes." She took the last bite, finishing the slice and catching a string of cheese on the pad of one finger. She licked that finger. Gage's groin tightened. He took her wrist gently and brought her hand to his mouth. "Let me do that."

Mallory held his gaze and nodded.

* * *

They made love again and again throughout the night. Gage couldn't seem to get enough of her and Mallory felt the same. She was sore in places that hadn't received this much attention in some time. And, she had to admit, a smile spreading across her lips, her places had never been attended to this well.

Gage was braced above her on one elbow. He reached out and ran his thumb across her grin. "You look—"

She laughed. "Give a woman multiple orgasms, multiple times and she's bound to look happy."

"I was about to say beautiful." He leaned down and kissed her, his lips warm and tender. "But, happy to oblige."

Unbelievably, the touch of his lips had her wanting him again.

He stretched. "I could use a shower."

He was off the bed in an instant, swooping her up into his arms. With a startled shriek, Mallory wound her arms around his neck.

She heard a beep. Her laptop was still on the coffee table in the living room and the beep signaled new email. Gage must have heard it too. He set her on her feet. They exchanged a look and then were both on the move.

Mallory looked at the message then up at Gage. "An ad for hair replacement."

"Hasn't been long since you posted the profiles," he said.

He was right but she was finding it hard to be patient with so much at stake.

Gage uncurled the fingers she'd unconsciously fisted, then took her hand and slowly brought her to her feet. He wrapped his arms around her.

Mallory closed her eyes and let herself lean on him. Gage tightened his hold.

* * *

The next evening, Mallory checked the dating sites again. She'd been checking at intervals that became shorter and shorter throughout the day. Gage handed her a sandwich and as she chewed, she registered that there still had been no responses. She wasn't certain that tracking down the other dancer would lead them to the missing girls and she felt that until/if she got a hit, she and Gage were just spinning their wheels.

Gage leaned over the back of the sofa. "Anything?"

"Zip."

She'd lost count of the number of times she'd checked her phone messages, hoping to find a call from York. She'd placed a call to him and learned that so far there'd been no sign of Billy. Wherever he'd holed up, he'd hidden himself well.

She hadn't received any more email since the hair replacement ad late last night. Following that, when anxiety and despair had weighed heavily on her, Gage had held her for a long time here in the living room, then eventually, moving her to the bed where he'd held her for the rest of the night. He'd given her his strength and his compassion when she'd needed them. She wasn't used to revealing her hurt so openly with anyone other than family, but with him, with Gage, it had felt acceptable to do so and more than that, it had felt right.

Gage picked up the keys to the rental from the coffee table. "All set?"

She nodded.

The last girl on their list was Rita Castile. The advertisement from six years earlier was for a club in the neighboring city of Crowley, approximately one hour away. They made good time due to the lateness of the hour and the resulting lack of traffic.

The club was a sharp contrast to the one they'd visited last night. The girl on the stage looked dated and less than enthusiastic about being there. No flashy costume or special effects lighting or accessories enhanced her performance. Other than Mallory herself and Gage, there were only two other customers in the place, both nursing mugs of beer.

This time they couldn't be circumspect about their reason for being at the club. Their

information about Rita Castile was too old for
that. Upon entering they approached the
bartender, and with a flash of ID, Mallory asked
to speak with the manager.

The manager, Mike Cooper, met them at the
bar. Mallory introduced herself and Gage, then
Cooper ushered them into his office. The room
looked as dingy and worn as the rest of the place.
Water stains darkened the tiled ceiling and cracks
split the linoleum floor. Mike himself was stick-
thin and sporting a bad comb-over.

Gage took a seat in front of Cooper's desk.
"We're looking for a dancer who worked here.
Rita Castile."

Cooper scratched his head. "Name's not
familiar. She's not working for me now. What do
you want with her?"

"Just want to have a word," Gage said.

Cooper slid his chair along the floor to a file
cabinet in one corner. The casters on the club feet
screeched as they connected with the worn
flooring. Cooper slid open a drawer and fingered
the contents.

"Had a Rita Castile working here. Six years
back. Whoa!" He chuckled. "That's going back a
ways."

Mallory addressed Cooper. "Were you the
manger here then?"

"Manager then and now. Owner then and
now. Got a note here that Rita left. Quit."

Mallory arched her brows. "Any reason why?"

"None that I thought important enough to
write down. Look six years is a long time ago.
People come, people go. That's how it is in this

business."

Gage pointed to the open folder. "What address do you have for Rita?"

Cooper recited it. Gage plucked a business card from a holder on Cooper's desk and jotted down the information. "Any of the dancers who worked with Rita still here?"

"Just one."

Gage glanced at Cooper. "We'd like to speak with her."

Cooper shrugged. "Why not."

He picked up the phone on his desk, an old fashioned rotary, and dialed an extension.

"Honey," he said a short time later, "can you come into my office? ... thanks." He replaced the phone. "She's on her way."

There was a knock on the door, then it opened and a woman entered the office. Lines had cut deep around her eyes and mouth, made more prominent by the thick application of garish make up.

"Amanda, these folks are from the police and the FBI," Cooper said. "They want to talk to you."

Amanda linked her fingers. "I don't know nothing that would interest the cops."

Mallory faced the other woman. "We're not here to talk about you, Amanda. We want to ask you about a woman who worked here a few years back. Rita Castile."

"Rita? What about Rita?"

Gage looked to Cooper. "Would you mind if we used your office while we speak with Amanda?"

"Sure. Go ahead. I got things to do anyway."

Amanda's gaze followed Cooper until he was out of sight and then lingered on the space he'd vacated. Her woeful expression conveyed apprehension, as if she'd been left on a sinking ship.

A phone somewhere outside the office began to ring as Mallory spoke. "How well did you know Rita?"

"Not well," Amanda shrugged and one sleeve of the sequined top she wore slid down her bony shoulder. "Well, a little well, I guess. We ate together sometimes away from work or went shopping. You know? Listen is Rita in some kind of trouble? Because if she is, I don't know nothing about that."

Mallory shook her head. "No trouble at all. We're trying to locate her. Do you know where we can find her?"

Amanda licked her lips. "No. We haven't been in touch since she left."

"Why did she leave?" Mallory asked.

"She got her Cinderella story. You know?" Another shrug that sent the sleeve down another inch. "Met a man. Got married. Lived happily ever after."

Gage rose from the chair and leaned back against Cooper's desk. "What was the man's name?"

Amanda scrunched up her face. "Can't remember it."

"Did Rita mention where she'd worked before coming here?" Mallory said.

"Not to me."

Mallory looked to Gage. He shook his head

once. "Okay, Amanda. Thanks for your time."

* * *

Back at her apartment, Mallory sat on the sofa in front of her laptop and logged onto the Bureau's database. She entered Rita Castile's name and her last known address. "No criminal record or hits of any kind. I'm going to search the DMV."

Gage came to stand beside her. "Failing that there's the IRS. Uncle Sam will be able to provide an address."

As it turned out, contacting the IRS wasn't necessary. The New York State Department of Motor Vehicles came back with several listings for drivers under that name.

Gage leaned over Mallory's shoulder. "DOB is too old for the first Rita to be the one we're looking for. Next one is too young."

They went through the listings, eliminating all but four.

"I'm going to cross reference these with marriages recorded six years ago." When the listings came up, Mallory scrolled through them slowly. "I think we hit pay dirt." She touched the computer screen. "Rita Freeman formerly Rita Castile. Here's an address." Mallory grabbed the notebook from her purse and wrote it down. "Not too far from here. We can drive over there in the morning." She got to her feet and took Gage's hand in hers. "Take me to bed."

He brushed a strand of hair from her face then kissed her tenderly, keeping their lips locked as he backed her out of the living room and to her bed. He eased her onto the mattress. While he slowly began to remove her clothing, his lips traveled as slowly over her face. Just that much contact had her burning for him, but it was clear that tonight he wouldn't be rushed.

"So pretty," he murmured. "Right here." He kissed the tip of her nose.

She would have laughed if she could have but he'd moved on to her neck and was now gently sucking and licking her pulse point. She'd never known that to be an erogenous zone but with him it had become one and she began to squirm.

She reached for him, undoing the buttons on his shirt. He was all contours and hard, hard muscle. If he thought her pretty, right back at you, Gage.

He was still taking off items of her clothing. He would have been finished by now. Really she wasn't wearing that much, but his progress was hampered by the soft, lingering caresses he gave each part of her that he uncovered. He paid complete, unhurried attention to every inch of her as it was revealed to him and now the fire he'd built grew to a blaze. As he put one hand on one breast and his hot, open mouth on the other, she forgot to breathe until the need for air overtook her.

She unzipped him, then nudged him to raise his hips so she could remove his jeans. His erection, hard and swollen, pressed against her thigh. She reached down and stroked him slowly, an easy up and down motion that had him clutching her to him and rubbing his forehead back and forth against her breast.

"You're killing me," he whispered.

Was she? She only knew what he was doing to her. She looked at him. His handsome features pulled taut. His body, muscles now tensed and with a slight sheen of perspiration. His erection growing bigger and harder. In response to what she was seeing, she felt another wave of desire.

She slid down his body to his arousal. As she took him into her mouth, he released a soft grunt. She took him deeper and he said something she didn't catch. She was too lost in him. Too near the edge.

He eased her from him and in a movement that came faster than his next breath, he lifted her, and rolled onto his back. His biceps bulging slightly, he held her above him. His eyes fixed on hers without blinking for one, two, then three wild beats of her heart. He brought her mouth to his and as he kissed her, hot and wet he lowered her slowly onto his erection.

Mallory gasped at the contact and she heard Gage hiss his next breath.

He put his large hands on her hips, gently lifting her, then lowering her again, guiding her in a rhythm that matched each stroke of his tongue against hers. As far gone as Mallory knew he was, she could feel his restraint. He was holding her back, keeping her from taking him in as deeply as she could, testing her readiness. She was beyond ready. She wanted more of him, all of him and urged him in further.

Finally, he complied and entered her completely. Mallory's eyes closed and she made a small plaintive sound into his mouth.

Gage increased their rhythm and Mallory eagerly kept pace. She gave herself over to the sensation, fisting her hands in his hair and she climaxed to Gage's own shout of release and his name echoing in her head.

They kissed softly, a tender caress of tongues, a gentle pressure of lips, then she let her face loll onto his neck. His arm came around her, holding her to him. Mallory slept.

* * *

Mallory looked at the paper she held and read the address. "This is the street, Gage."

It was just after nine in the morning. They were on the road Rita Castile Freeman lived on. A garbage truck lumbered down the street, making its rounds. Gage fell in behind the truck as Mallory checked house numbers.

"Forty nine. Fifty one. That one. Number fifty three." Mallory pointed to a neat semi-detached house painted a pretty golden shade. There wasn't a car in the single driveway, but Gage parked at the curb and they left the vehicle.

The driveway had been cleared of snow, but flakes dusted the small front lawn and sprinkled the eavestrough and shutters.

Mallory rang the front door bell. The sound carried to the porch from inside the house, a sing song chime. The door was opened almost at once.

"So what did you forget?"

The smiling woman who opened the door was an older and softer version of the Rita Castile they'd viewed on the club advertisement. Her face was scrubbed clean of cosmetics. Her hair was cut short in a sassy bob that swung as she tilted her head to one side. She braced the door with one hand and rested the other on her very pregnant abdomen.

"Oh, hi." Rita smiled. "I was expecting my husband. He just left and I thought he came back because he forgot something. But you're not him. Obviously. Can I help you?"

Mallory showed her ID and Rita blanched. "I'm Agent Burke and this is Captain Broderick. We just want a couple of minutes of your time. May we come in?"

Rita swallowed visibly, clearly uncomfortable with the request but she backed away from the door. "Yeah. Okay."

They entered a small hall painted a cheery pink. Small plaques that depicted cartoon characters hung on one wall. On the other, a trio of framed embroidered cloths were centered. The largest embroidery of the three was a house with the caption "Home Sweet Home" beneath.

Rita linked her hands. "Come in to the living room."

The floral theme and homey atmosphere continued in there. A large glass vase was filled with perky yellow daisies.

Gage and Mallory took places on a yellow couch. Rita perched on the end of a matching chair, her hands now clasped tightly around her stomach. Eyes wide, she watched Mallory then Gage in turn, her distress evident.

Mallory resisted the urge to reassure Rita. She

had a job to do. Without preamble, she got to the reason for their visit. "Did you ever work at The Wild Club, Rita?" Mallory didn't think it was possible for Rita to get any paler, but she did.

"How did you find me? Please, I'm married now. I'm having a baby." She rubbed circles around her stomach. "My husband doesn't know about that part of my life. That I was a dancer. He's very conservative. He can't find out about that. It would end my marriage."

"We don't have any intention of speaking with your husband," Mallory said. "We just need to get some information from you. That's all. How long did you work at The Wild Club?"

"Seven, eight months."

"Did Billy Wilder hire you?"

Rita gnawed her bottom lip. "Aha."

"Why did you leave the club?"

Rita smoothed an embroidered cushion, then took the fringe between her fingertips and began to pleat the material. "It was a long time ago. A life time ago for me. What can it matter now?"

Mallory kept her response vague. "It may matter a great deal, Rita. Go on."

Rita licked her lips. "Billy arranged private parties."

"Private parties?"

Rita nodded. "He'd invite a few of the girls, the dancers, saying that the tips would be more than we'd earn dancing in a month."

"Did you ever go to any of these parties?"

In a near whisper she said, "I went to one."

Mallory curled her fingers around the strap of her purse. "What went on at these parties?"

"Dancing for the male guests, then each guy would take one or more of the girls in to one of the rooms in back to party in private."

"To have sex, you mean?"

Rita gave a slow up and down motion with her head.

"Were all the dancers from Billy's club?" Mallory said.

Rita lifted the pillow out of her lap and hugged it to her chest. "Not to the one I went. I was the only one."

Gage had been quietly observing but spoke up now. "What happened after that party?"

Rita turned wide, fearful eyes on Gage. "We were all driven home. That was it."

The garbage truck stopped at the curb in front of Rita's house. The motor grinded. Mallory waited out the loud noise, taking in Rita's information, then resumed the interview. "How long were you working at the club before you went to that party?"

Rita cleared her throat. "I was new, just there a few weeks. I went mostly cause I didn't want to make Billy mad and look like I didn't want to fit in. I really needed the job."

"So you stayed on working at the club after that party?"

She nodded.

"What changed that made you quit work there?" Gage said.

Rita swallowed. "Billy hosted another party, but he didn't ask me to that one. I figured he was looking for blondes because he asked only the blond girls and I never told him I didn't want to go again. Like I said, I needed the job." She took a breath, let it out slowly. "There was another girl who started working there. She was new, like me, and we kinda became friends. Billy invited her, that's how I heard about it. Billy was real hush hush about this party. He'd never been that way about the other one. The new girl, Caitlin, thought the whole mystery thing was a kick. She jumped at the chance to make extra money. I told her what went down at the party I went to, and that we were expected to put out, but Caitlin said she could take care of herself and went anyway."

Rita stopped speaking.

"What happened at that party?" Gage prodded gently.

Rita's eyes filled with tears. "I don't know."

"Caitlin didn't tell you?" Mallory said.

"I never saw Caitlin again."

Mallory leaned forward. "What do you mean?"

"She never came back to work after that night."

Mallory felt a tightness in her stomach. "Did you ask Billy about her?"

"When she didn't show up for work the day after the party, I asked Billy if she was sick. He told me she'd cleared out. Quit."

"You didn't believe him?"

Rita shook her head. "I knew where Caitlin lived. She rented a room not far from the club and I went there. Her land lady told me a man came by, said he was Caitlin's brother. He paid the bill for her rent. Took her things. Said that Caitlin wouldn't be back. She was moving back home with her family."

"You don't think that's what happened?" Mallory said.

"She had a bad home life, same as me. Left home and wouldn't go back. And, she didn't have a brother. I told the land lady that, but she said I must have made a mistake and that was that. I knew some of the other girls had also gone to that party with Caitlin, so I asked them if they left with her. They said they had. That they'd all left together. Same as always. But it wasn't the same. Caitlin was gone."

Mallory felt saddened at Rita's response and renewed anger at Billy and Considine. "Did you go to the police?"

Rita laughed without humor. "Are you kidding? I was a stripper and a prostitute thanks to that one party. People like me don't go to the police. The police aren't friends to people like me. But Caitlin was my friend. I had to do something. I told Billy that I was afraid something happened to Caitlin at that party. He told me I did the right thing by coming to him. That the safety of his girls is all important and he'd check this out. The day after I talked to him, though, things started happening to me."

Mallory frowned. "What kinds of things?"

"Crank calls. Hang ups and breathers. Then, one night, I got locked in the laundry room at my apartment building. The lights went out and a man grabbed me, put a knife to my throat. I thought I was going to die." Her voice broke. "Someone started banging on the door, wanting to come in and wash her own clothes. The guy went out through the utility door." She closed her eyes. Tears leaked from the corners. "I couldn't prove that Billy was behind that, but I never went back to the club. Didn't even pick up my last pay check. I left the city, got a job in a run down out of the way club."

Cooper's club, Mallory thought.

Rita was crying openly now. Mallory took a box of tissues from an end table and held it out to the other woman. She plucked one and held it to her eyes.

"You can't go bringing all this up again." Rita's voice was choked with tears. "Like I said, my husband doesn't know about what I did before we got married."

Rita began to sob and rock.

"Rita, look at me." Mallory wasn't sure the woman heard her as the tissue remained pressed to her eyes and she continued her back and forth movement. "Rita?" This time Rita lowered the tissue and Mallory attempted to calm the woman. "We have no reason to speak with your husband. No reason. Okay?"

After a moment of eye contact, Rita nodded.

"What was Caitlin's last name, Rita?" Mallory said.

"Dell."

"Did she say where she was from?"

"Midwest, I think."

Not a local girl and Mallory wondered if Considine's trafficking business extended to other states. "What did you hear about the party she went to?"

"What do you mean? Nothing. I told you, she never made it back."

"Who else was invited?" Mallory clarified. "Where was it held?"

"A couple of girls from the club. I don't remember who." Rita bunched the tissue in her fist. "As for the men invited, guest list was private. I don't even know the name of the man I was with when I partied."

"Think, Rita." Mallory slid to the end of the sofa, reducing the distance to the other woman. "Maybe you'll remember something more. It's important."

"I think Caitlin said she heard Billy talking and that the party was going to be on a boat, a yacht. Yeah, I think that's it. She was excited about that. Said she'd never been on a yacht before."

"What about the name of the yacht? Did she mention that?"

Rita dabbed her eyes with the tissue. "I doubt she knew. The way things worked, we were picked up, driven to the destination, only finding out where when we got there. I never saw her again." Rita choked on fresh tears.

Mallory placed her hand on Rita's. "Are you going to be all right? Do you need us to stay with you for a while or is there someone we can call to come stay with you?"

Rita removed her hand from Mallory's. "Please just go and don't ever come back."

* * *

On the walk back to the car, Mallory raised the hood of her jacket and stuck her hands deep into her jacket pockets to stave off the chill. None of that helped. Her talk with Rita had left her with a coldness that ran bone deep. "Caitlin Dell. I want to run her through the system. See if anything turns up."

Gage put his arm around her shoulders and drew her to his side. "I'd be surprised if anything does. Sounds like Wilder didn't miss a step to keep those parties under wraps."

Inside her jacket pockets, Mallory's fists clenched. "He just can't keep getting away with this, Gage. We have to stop him and then through him, Considine."

They returned to her apartment. After they'd performed what had become their usual check of the place, she logged onto the Bureau's database and entered Caitlin Dell's name. "You were right, Gage. Nothing came back on Caitlin."

"Wilder and Considine were sure to know that," Gage said. "She was easy prey."

"No one was even looking for her." Mallory stared at the screen and felt a deep sadness over that.

In her haste to follow up on Caitlin, Mallory hadn't removed her jacket when she'd entered the apartment. Gage slid down the zipper and tugged one sleeve off. Turning away from that blank screen she removed the other, then hung the jacket in the closet.

She heard a small beep from her laptop. She went still at the sound. A message? Plopping down in front of her computer again, she saw it. She blinked to make sure that her mind hadn't conjured the email, so desperate was she for there to be one. But, no, her eyes weren't playing tricks.

"Gage."

He came up behind her and put his hands on her shoulders. "What does the message say?"

"Basic greeting. Brief bio. Into weight lifting and body building. Rap music. Having a good time."

She typed back a description that continued the traits exhibited by the girls in Wilder's photos and added the reminder that she was nineteen and into music and fun." She hit send.

Within a few minutes, she received a response. The exchange continued into the early afternoon.

"I'm so tempted to ask to meet," Mallory said.

"Need to wait for him to initiate contact."

"I know you're right but I'm so tired of waiting. Another message." She sat up straighter as she read. "Bingo. A request to meet."

"Where?"

"Not there yet. He's waiting for me to agree." Mallory typed *Yes* then hit send.

This time the response held a specific location. She read aloud. "Grandview Park. At the fountain. Four p.m. Will bring the beer." Mallory replied "See You" with an abbreviated *C U*.

"Do you know where Grandview Park is?" Gage said.

"Next county."

"With the weather, won't be many people there."

She glanced out the window at the dull sky heavy with clouds promising more snow. "A good isolated choice."

"How long to get there?"

"Half hour, I'd say."

"You familiar with the place?" Gage asked.

"Never been there."

"Do a search. Bring it up on screen. I want to see if there's a layout of the area."

She tapped the keyboard, bringing up a website. Gage sat beside her, clicking on the links. There weren't many of them and fewer visuals. Mostly, the write-ups touted the natural beauty of the place and the couple of photos showed sprawling green grass under a blazing sun.

Gage took his hand from the laptop. "That was no help to us. If this guy is the one we're looking for, he'll get there ahead of the meet time, wanting to set himself up. Box you in so you won't be able to make a run for it when he makes his move. I want to get there before him. Look the place over. Make sure we can cover you." Gage checked his watch. "We should leave now."

* * *

Gage parked on the street, a short distance away from the park between an SUV and a white van and they left the car. The sky had grown darker during the drive here. Mallory looked up at the sky laden with clouds and hoped the snow dump would wait a little longer.

At the entrance to the park, a wooden board held a map of the place. Mallory traced her finger along a thin red line. "By the look of this, the fountain is off a path, into the trees. Away from the main stream of things."

Gage grunted at that. He took her hand and led her onto the snow covered grounds.

The crunch of snow beneath their steps sounded louder than it should have due to the absence of other sounds.

"This place is deserted," Mallory said. "Not even a bird or squirrel."

Gage looked around, then back over his shoulder. "So far, the only exit point I've seen is back the way we came."

"The path forks up ahead. That could be another way in or out of here."

"Our guy could approach from that fork." Gage rolled his shoulders. "Let's see if that path also ends at the fountain."

They cleared a stand of Evergreens. A large cement fountain rose up out of a small clearing. It was dry, turned off for the winter. A wooden bench sat a few feet in front of six statues of ducks swimming in a row.

They hung back, under the cover of the trees, taking in their surroundings. There wasn't anyone in the clearing and if the guy they were after was in the dense trees behind the fountain, it was impossible to tell. The upside to that was he couldn't see them either.

Mallory slid her hand from Gage's. "I can't stand here and wait for him to show first. I need to act like a woman hot for this date. I'm going ahead."

She could see from his expression that Gage didn't like it, but that was the reason they were in this park, freezing their assess off and he nodded. As she stepped away from him, he held her arm. "Take no chances."

Mallory nodded and entered the clearing. Her

hand was in her coat pocket, gripping her gun.

The wind toyed with her hair, blowing it across her eyes, but she resisted the urge to loop it behind her ears and bare her face. She didn't want whoever was coming to realize she didn't look like the photograph she'd posted until it was too late.

She checked her watch. It was a couple of minutes before four. A few more minutes passed, then she heard a rustling sound and a man appeared on the path. He was dressed in a hoodie that was pulled over his head with a ball cap beneath. The brim cast his face in shadow and she couldn't make out his features. Whoever this was, he'd lied on his profile that he was a body builder. The guy was thin as a bean pole. Not that his appearance was of any concern at this point, once he'd lured his prey. He was also carrying a six pack of beer.

The guy breezed past where Gage was hiding in the trees and toward her, his stride long and lanky. He stopped in front of her and Mallory got her first look at his face. He'd claimed to be twenty one in his email message and looked like he'd reached that age about five minutes ago. He had an unfortunate beak nose and a severe case of acne that he tried to cover up by not shaving. As a result, whiskers had sprouted and formed patches on his face that looked like weeds.

He smiled. "Hey, I'm Kyle."

She gave him a show of teeth in return. "Hey, Kyle."

On the surface it appeared this kid really was expecting to meet a date, but Mallory knew appearances could deceive and she made a decision to play this out a little longer. She wanted to make sure this wasn't a slick set up before she cut the kid loose, that this boy wasn't a front for someone else who would swoop in like a vulture and nab an unsuspecting girl.

"Brought the beer." Kyle held up the pack. "Let's party."

He went to the wooden bench, brushed off the snow on the seat with the beer cans, then slumped against the back, trying to look cool, it appeared to Mallory. He slid on the bench, ruining the pose. Some heat crept into his cheeks and he tried again. This time he got it down.

"Come and sit." He held out his hand in invitation.

When she didn't comply, he added, 'please' in a voice that squeaked.

Mallory lowered herself onto the bench. Kyle popped the tops off two cans of beer, placed one on the seat beside her, then draped his arm along the back of the bench. The smell of beer mingled with whatever cologne he'd liberally used and underlying perspiration.

He took a long swig. "Drink up. Got plenty more."

The snow started. A few flakes landed on her eyelashes. Ignoring them, she trained her gaze on the boy. "How long have you been on that dating site?"

"Not long. Won't be going back now that I met you."

Mallory refrained from rolling her eyes. Could this be as innocent as it looked? Some kid looking to make out with a girl who was agreeable? She cautioned herself again that this could all be a ruse. That someone sinister could be waiting in the wings.

"You meet many girls there?"

The kid's arm landed on her shoulders. "None that mattered before you, babe."

Mallory shrugged his arm off of her. "How'd you find out about that site?"

His expression fell at her subtle rebuff with the shoulder. He took another swallow of beer. "Don't know. Around."

Kyle gave Mallory his version of a mega watt smile. "Enough talk. How 'bout we get busy?"

"Got anyone else coming?"

The kid's lips turned down at the corners in a pout. "No worries, babe. I'm more than enough man for you."

He leaned in for a kiss and Mallory slapped her palm on the kid's chest, pushing him back. "I'm out of here."

She stood, but didn't walk away. This would be the point where Kyle would signal to someone else for help to detain her, but, in truth, she wasn't expecting it. Nor was she expecting Kyle to suggest moving on to another location to save the evening, or to make some move on his own to detain her forcefully now that his attempt at seduction had gone south. And she was right, the kid flopped back against the seat as docile as a puppy.

"But I bought beer?" he murmured.

Mallory glanced back over her shoulder. "Consider it a bad investment."

"Strike one," Gage said when she joined him in the trees.

CHAPTER NINE

Mallory unlocked the door to her apartment. When she was about to step inside, Gage placed a hand on her arm.

She should have been used to this routine of checking out the place by now. They'd performed it each time they returned to her apartment, but this time it grated as no time before had. After they were sure they were alone, Mallory scrolled through her phone messages. None from York. She released a quick, tense breath. Next she checked her profile pages for any other hits. Nothing. She closed the lid of her laptop with a snap so loud it brought Gage's head around.

"You okay?" he said.

"Fine."

Gage rubbed the back of his neck. "I'm going to hit the shower, then we'll do something about dinner." When she didn't respond, he said, "Mallory?"

She looked up at him and nodded.

He watched her a moment longer, then left the living room.

Waiting for York to pick up Billy was going nowhere. In the meantime, Considine was free to conduct his business as usual. She felt as if the women were slipping away. So much time had passed and still, they had nothing. It was time she turned nothing into something.

Gage.

She listened for the sound of the shower then penned a note to him.

Went out.

* * *

Paul Considine owned a couple of night clubs in Manhattan. Clubs that were completely legitimate. Mallory had never been to one of Considine's clubs but as she went through the double glass doors, she saw that the hype hadn't exaggerated. The decor was posh with glittering chandeliers and expensive rugs over marble floors.

The club boasted upscale entertainment with shows that featured top dancers, singers, and comedians where it was rumored even top government officials had been known to bring their spouses.

One more thing the club had, and the thing Mallory was most interested in, were the security cameras. They were everywhere and though discreet so as not to be eye sores, they were visible. Mallory went to the bar in one of several restaurants that made up a part of this club.

Spotting one of the cameras, she went to stand beneath it. She tilted her head back so her full face was exposed. *Smile.*

Three hours later, she'd made the rounds of both of Considine's clubs, always sure to stroll beneath the eyes of the lens. Satisfied that she'd splashed her face around enough, she went home.

As soon as she inserted her key in the lock, Gage pulled the door open so abruptly she grabbed the wall to regain her balance.

She returned her arm to her side. "Hello."

His gaze sharpened as he looked at her, taking her in. His face was stark with worry. "Are you all right?"

She felt a stab of guilt at that, but she didn't regret what she'd done. "I'm sorry if I worried you."

"*If* you worried me?"

"*That* I worried you," she amended.

He rubbed a hand down his face and blew out a long breath. "Where did you go? And why did you go without me?"

Mallory closed the door slowly. The soft thud hung in the air as she took a moment to respond. "I went to Considine's clubs."

"You went where?" Gage shook his head as if he hadn't heard her right or comprehended the words.

"Paul Considine has two clubs in the city. I went to both of them."

Gage's eyes slitted. "We've been doing all we can to keep you safe from Considine and you're telling me that tonight you went to him?"

His tone had Mallory straightening her spine. "Not to him. To his places of business."

Gage clenched his jaw. "What—to flaunt yourself under his nose?"

She crossed her arms. "It wasn't like that."

"Wasn't it? Then why didn't you take me with you?"

Mallory lifted her chin but remained silent.

Gage grasped her shoulders. "I'll tell you why, because you wanted him to focus solely on you."

"I want Considine to feel heat. He's not getting enough of that. If he starts to feel pressured, he'll make a mistake. Maybe one we can use to find the women."

Gage's grip on her tightened. "Are you out of your mind?"

"In case you've forgotten, I'm a trained agent."

"Is that what the feds teach? To pull stunts like this one?"

Mallory glared at him. "I know what I'm doing."

His eyes went so dark, she saw her own reflection. "I'm not going to stand by and watch you take unnecessary risks."

"That's not what I'm doing."

"The hell it's not. You're going to get yourself killed."

She could feel heat coming off him, a combination of anger and frustration. She was feeling the same, though in her case, anger won out. "That's not going to happen."

His body tensed. The muscles in his shoulders and arms strained. "No, it's not. Not on my watch."

She leaned toward him and tilted her head all the way back to look up at him. With the significant differences in their height, it was the closest she could come to getting in his face. "We're no longer at the cabin. I'm not on *your* watch."

She shoved his shoulder. He stepped back.

* * *

Mallory spent the time since her fight with Gage in her bedroom with her laptop. Angry. Sulking. No, not sulking. Well, maybe. Gage had inadvertently struck a nerve.

With a long, drawn out sigh, she set the laptop onto her nightstand and went to find him.

He was at the window. The snow had stopped and outside the sky was dark but for the city lights twinkling.

"You were right before," she said.

He turned and faced her. "Right?"

"When you said that I deliberately didn't take you with me to Considine's clubs. I did want him to see just me rather than both of us. I wanted to show him that he hadn't intimidated me. That I would not allow him to intimidate me. To control me. I needed to prove that to myself."

Gage put his arms tight around her and drew her up onto her toes. "You don't have anything to prove to anyone." He kissed her as if it had been years rather than hours. Mallory clutched his wrists, feeling the same.

A thud came from outside in the hall. Gage pushed her behind him and removed his gun from the small of his back. Mallory's purse was on the table and she withdrew her own gun. Gage took up a position to one side of the door. Sound carried from the hallway. A woman's voice then another.

"Here let me help you, Mary."

"Thanks."

Not the sound of assassins, Mallory thought.

"I don't know why they don't double bag the heavy stuff. This always happens."

Gage peered out through the peep hole, then turned away from the door and returned his gun to the back of his jeans. "Two women. Crouched over an assortment of cans and jars on the carpeting."

"Just a woman who dropped her groceries." Mallory felt relief at that and then anger. "I hate this. I hate jumping at every sound. What did I tell you about not wanting to let Considine intimidate me." She set her weapon on the coffee table, then pushed her now slightly damp bangs off her brow. "If he could see me now."

Gage went to her and took one of her hands in his own. "You'd be an idiot not to be afraid. Not to be on your guard."

"This is personal between me and Considine."

"Personal, how?"

Mallory drew a deep breath. "The summer I graduated from high school, I took a five day trip to Manhattan. Me and Cassie, my best friend." Mallory shook her head slowly. "Best friends doesn't adequately describe how we felt about each other. Cassie and I weren't related by blood but she was my sister in every way that mattered.

We were done with finals and wanted to blow off steam. We were set to start college a couple of months later and wanted to kick up our heels before we had to buckle down." Mallory paused. "The night before we were due to go home, Cassie disappeared."

Gage squeezed her hand. "What happened?"

"We were doing the club thing. Having a good time going from club to club. We wanted to hit as many as we could in the time we were in New York. So we could say, hey, we'd been there. We weren't drinking heavily. We both knew to keep our wits about us and we weren't looking to pick up anyone for more than just a dance or two. It was fun. Harmless. Before we'd gone out that night, as we had on the previous nights, we'd said that we wouldn't separate." Mallory lowered her head. "But we did get separated. The crowd thickened and I lost sight of her. I didn't think much of it at first. I figured she was somewhere in the club. I took out my cell phone and called her. Her cell went to voice mail. Not surprising if she couldn't hear her phone ringing with all the noise. I began making my way through the mob, looking for her. But an hour later, I couldn't find her."

Mallory's throat closed as memories of that night returned and emotion swamped her. "I checked the restrooms and then went to check outside the club, in case for some reason she'd stepped out there. When I didn't find her, I waited. Eventually, she would need to leave there. I kept trying her cell. She never picked up. The crowd eventually thinned as the night wore on and I checked inside the club again. At that point, it wasn't hard to see that Cassie wasn't in there."

Mallory swiped a tear that fell onto her cheek. "The cop who took my frantic call told me that unless I had evidence of foul play, he couldn't file a missing persons report for forty eight hours. Cassie was nineteen. An adult. She could come and go as she pleased. He suggested that she'd met someone and would return soon. He asked me if I'd been back to our hotel. I hadn't and he suggested I check back there. She wasn't at the hotel."

Mallory's voice cracked. She cleared her throat. "I called home. Cassie's parents and my parents flew in from Chicago. An investigation began, but Cassie wasn't found.

"Months went by without any word. I missed that year of college. After she disappeared, each time the phone rang or a car pulled into our driveway, I was terrified that her body had been found. I know most people want to know what happened when a loved one disappears, but for me as long as no body turned up, I could hold onto the hope that she'd be found and brought home.

"And then one day the call I'd been fearing came. Cassie's body had been discovered. Her identity confirmed. She was found in a city in Asia. In a Dumpster."

Gage brought her against his chest. He pressed his lips to the top of her head. "I'm sorry, baby."

Mallory put her arms around Gage's waist. Her eyes welled with tears, soaking into his shirt. "Cassie had been a victim of human traffickers and sold into slavery."

"Were her traffickers ever caught?"

Mallory swallowed to clear the tears that clogged her throat. "To this day, we don't know who trafficked her or who she was sold to. Her killer was never found."

"That's why you've been tracking the disappearances of young women all these years," Gage said gently. "You're trying to find the people who sold Cassie."

She didn't answer. She didn't have to. He knew that he'd drawn the correct conclusion.

She raised her head from his chest and looked up at him. "And now, I finally have a lead to a human trafficking operation."

"You think Considine is the one who abducted Cassie." Gage said it as a statement not a question.

"Yes. I can't let him do the same to those twelve women. I won't."

Gage took her face gently between his broad palms. "You're doing all that can be done. Wilder will be apprehended and through him, Considine. Because of you, Considine's operation will be shut down."

Mallory swallowed the last of the tears and straightened her spine. "It has to go down that way, Gage. He has to be made to pay for what he did to Cassie. I have to give that closure to her parents. I need it for myself."

His eyes became shadowed. "I hope having that gives you what you need."

She sensed they were no longer talking about her. "Why were you at the cabin, Gage?"

He lowered his arms, releasing her. "Let it go, Mallory."

"I would, if you could."

He was silent for so long, Mallory was afraid he would remain so, but he began to speak. "Six months ago, I was working on a case involving a drug cartel. The bust was big and we arrested several top people including the guy who ran the operation. During his arrest, the leader opened fire. Took down a couple of our guys. I took him out.

"It was a clean kill. Internal Affairs cleared me. Used necessary force, etcetera. The guy I shot had a brother who was his second in command. The brother got away before we could arrest him. We couldn't find any trace of him and with his business severely crippled, if not entirely wiped out, we believed he'd left the country for parts unknown. I believed that."

Gage's features went taut. His brows lowered over his eyes that darkened with pain. "I was married at one time. My ex-wife and I have been divorced for longer than the marriage lasted, but out of that mess we got twin boys. It was my weekend with them. The boys wanted to go to the zoo. I never saw it coming. One minute we were watching the monkeys and the next my sons were on the ground, bleeding. Dying."

"Gage . . "

He shuddered and bent his head. He fell silent, his throat working. "The brother of the man I'd killed was the one who shot my sons. I shot and killed him right after he fired those two shots, but it was already too late. Ben and Josh died instantly. They were four years old."

Tears fell onto Mallory's cheeks. "I'm so sorry, Gage."

"After my sons were killed, I couldn't do the job anymore. Didn't want to. I didn't want to be around anyone. Mitch had a cabin he used during summer months. He offered it to me for as long as I wanted it. I closed up my house in Washington. Would have resigned my position with the police department, but my superior wouldn't accept my resignation. Gave me leave instead." Gage closed his eyes briefly. When he opened them, his expression was so pained, so raw, it took her breath. He stared directly into her eyes. "My call. My lapse in judgment cost my son's lives."

Mallory's voice broke along with her heart. "What happened wasn't your fault, Gage."

Her cell phone rang. Once. Twice. She allowed it to ring and put her arms around him.

He stiffened. "You should get that."

Mallory didn't answer the phone and she didn't release him.

"You need to get that," he said.

Not wanting to crowd him, Mallory took the call. It was York. Billy Wilder was in custody.

CHAPTER TEN

A light rain was falling, turning the snow on the ground to slush when they left Mallory's apartment. Gage activated the windshield wipers and in the absence of conversation, the swish swish of the blades moving across the glass became the dominant sound in the car.

He pulled in to the lot of the Bureau office. Mallory popped the door latch, then noticed he hadn't done the same. "Aren't you coming in? This is what we've been waiting for." But she noticed his expression was grim and she felt a frisson of alarm. "Gage?"

"I'm going to park the car here for you and take a cab to pick up the truck."

She nodded slowly. "Okay, but I can drive you once this is done with Wilder."

"I'm picking up the truck and driving to the cabin right after. Now that Wilder is in custody, Considine will have no reason to come after you. You're safe."

Which meant his job here was done. She hadn't wanted to crowd him earlier, but he'd already withdrawn. "Gage, let's talk about this."

"There's nothing to say."

"Being alone on the mountain isn't the answer."

"It's the only answer I've got."

Gage watched her without blinking, then leaned toward her and kissed her briefly. "They're waiting for you." He leaned across her and gave her door a shove.

Mallory stared at him for a long moment. She left the car before the tears burning her eyes welled and he'd see them. She barely made it through the door when the tears spilled onto her cheeks.

"Mallory, hold up!"

It was Special Agent Tom Cole, who'd also participated in the raid on the warehouse calling out to her now. Mallory swiped the back of her hand over her eyes, drying them.

Tom was at the other end of the lobby and jogged to her. "You here to watch Wilder being questioned?"

"Headed there now," she said.

Tom pushed his glasses up the bridge of his nose. "Me, too. I have some time before another appointment and I want to catch some of this. I'll ride up with you."

When they reached the interrogation room, Mallory was surprised to find the room was empty.

Tom put his hands on his hips. "No one's here yet."

They waited in the hall for York to arrive. Forty minutes later, they were still waiting.

Tom glanced at his watch. "That's it for me. Enjoy the show."

Another ten minutes passed and Mallory was still waiting. Had the questioning been delayed?

She took the elevator to York's office. Jane, the woman who had been York's assistant since Mallory was assigned to him was at her desk. "Is he in, Jane?"

"Yes. I'll let him know you'd like a word with him."

Again, Mallory was left to wait.

"How about a coffee while you're waiting?" Jane offered.

Mallory didn't think her nerves needed the added boost of caffeine and shook her head. "No, thanks."

Jane's phone buzzed. She took the call then said to Mallory. "Go on in."

Mallory pushed off the wall and entered the office. York was seated at his desk. His heavy jowls were more pronounced by the tight set to his mouth.

Mallory got right to the point. "What's happening with Wilder's interrogation, sir?"

York uttered a sound of disgust. "There isn't going to be any interrogation. Wilder was found dead in his cell in lock up."

"How did this happen?"

"Don't think I haven't been asking the same question of everyone in the holding block. All that is known so far is that Wilder was found hanging in his cell. At this point we don't know if it was a suicide or if he was murdered. I'll let you know what our people find out."

* * *

The Don felt his control slipping and it was because of the woman. Agent Mallory Burke. She'd survived his people's attack on the mountain and survived the fire.

He went to the drinks cart in his den and splashed a liberal dose of Scotch into a crystal glass then tossed it back. He poured another.

At this point, his original reason for pursuing her no longer applied. If it was just to prevent her from divulging what she'd learned of his organization when she'd insinuated herself at the club, that was now a moot point. She'd had ample time to give a full report to her superiors. His precaution of moving the women had been right. Without them there was nothing to prove an allegation of human trafficking. And now that he'd had that fool Wilder eliminated, her only known link to the Don had been severed.

But she was investigating other avenues. She'd learned nothing of any significance yet, but if she continued to dig, it was likely she would. The woman was dogged. Relentless in her pursuit. He had no doubt she would go on digging.

So far, she'd eluded him. Played him for a fool. His grip on the glass tightened and his knuckles whitened. No one played him for a fool.

She would learn that lesson soon. A lesson she would take to her grave.

CHAPTER ELEVEN

Mallory let herself into her apartment. The trail to the women had gone cold with Billy's death. Though they had no proof, Mallory laid the blame squarely at Considine's door. Considine hadn't let Billy live to tell what he knew.

Another day over and they were no closer to finding the women. She tossed her purse on the kitchen counter in a mild display of the frustration and helplessness she was feeling.

All she had were the dating sites. She was at a standstill with nowhere to go from here until/if one of them made contact.

She would have liked to be able to talk this out with Gage. He was a skilled investigator. She welcomed his input. And, she wanted his arms around her. Wanted his strength. His comfort. His touch.

She didn't want to recall making love with Gage, knowing all she would ever have were memories. She closed her eyes, trying to contain the images, but they would not be contained. They remained front and center in her mind and with them, her feelings for him. Impossible to ignore, they made her yearn for something she would never have.

She'd fallen in love with him. He didn't return her feelings. What he felt for her was a sense of responsibility. He'd made himself responsible for her safety and as soon as Billy Wilder was arrested and the threat to her from Considine was gone, Gage had left. Once she was out of danger, Gage's job was done.

He was so hurt, so closed-off. Pain and guilt had a choke-hold on him that he could not break. No doubt he would have blamed himself if Considine had harmed her. He couldn't carry any more guilt. He was bowing under a weight of blame for the death of his sons. She didn't know what to do about that. Tears stung her eyes.

The phone in her kitchen rang. Mallory snatched a tissue and wiped her eyes as she picked up the receiver. After her greeting a man apologized for dialing a wrong number.

"It's okay," she said in a monotone. She replaced the phone on the wall mount.

Her thoughts returned to Gage. Overwhelming her. Overpowering her. She slid down the wall to the floor and cried.

After, she picked herself up off the kitchen floor and went into the bathroom. She washed her face, pressing the damp cloth to her eyes. There would be more tears later but for now she had a job to do.

Considine had a weak spot. Somewhere. She

was going to find it.

She was returning to the kitchen when her front door burst open. Two men charged inside. Her purse was on the counter; her service weapon inside.

Ignoring the pain in her ankle, Mallory ran. She lunged for her purse but before she could reach her gun, she was pulled back by the hair. She reared back with her elbow, jabbing the big brute who held her in the sternum. His breath whooshed out and he released her. The man cursed. His was the voice from the wrong number. The hair on the back of Mallory's neck rose. This was no random break in. She was the target.

She was fighting for her life now. She spun away from the brute but the other man with him struck out with his fist and Mallory tasted blood. She landed a solid hit, then the brute recovered and grabbed her from behind. The man she'd struck knocked her to the floor, and kicked her in the side. She felt something break. He kicked her in the head and then she felt nothing at all.

* * *

Gage spent his first day back at the cabin attending to chores. Without the generator, the food in the fridge and freezer had spoiled. He'd anticipated that and had stopped for supplies on the drive up. He'd used most of the wood in the crate on the last night he and Mallory had spent here and was now outside, splitting logs.

The air was crisp and fresh. Snow glittered like

crystal in the bright sunlight and crunched under Gage's boots as he made his way over it to the shed for more wood to cut. All trace of what had gone down here with Considine's men was gone. There was nothing but snow as far as his eye could see. He suspected it would take some time for the creatures that lived on this mountain to venture out from wherever they'd taken refuge during the storm.

He'd come to these mountains seeking refuge but the mountains hadn't been able to give that to him. Nothing could.

Mallory.

Her name flashed in his mind.

He rolled his shoulders, now feeling on edge. Restless. The mountain, despite its wide open space felt oppressive. Dropping the ax atop the wood pile, he went into the cabin for the keys to Mitch's truck. He needed to get away from here for a while. He'd take a walk down the mountain and a trip into town, maybe for more supplies. Though he couldn't think what, he must have forgotten to get something.

Main Street was quiet when he drove into town. It was a work day and traffic, both pedestrian and vehicular was light. On impulse, he parked in front of the bar at the end of the street and went inside.

A few locals were shooting pool in a corner. A couple others sat at scarred wooden tables, drinking drafts and talking sports. Gage didn't know any of them which saved him from having to exchange greetings which was fine with him. He was in no mood to socialize. Just what his mood was, though, he couldn't say.

He ordered a beer and took the bottle to one of the booths in back. The solid thwack of one billiard ball striking another and sending it spinning into a corner pocket prompted a hoot from the man who'd made the shot. Sweet shot. Gage had to agree.

Gage was a decent pool player, himself. He wondered if Mallory played. He imagined her bending over the table, lining up a shot. Her features pulled taut in concentration. Her eyes narrowed and unblinking in their focus. She would give her all to the game, just as she gave her all to everything she did.

Gage shifted position on the bench and focused on the pool table. The game was over. The men were now engaging in a round of back slapping as they returned their cues. Without the distraction of their game, Gage sought another.

A TV was mounted on the wall above the bar. Tuned to a game show. Though only one of the bar stools was occupied, he remained standing and watched a contestant jump and squeal as the host congratulated her on being the winner. The credits rolled. The show ended.

He'd helped Mallory when she'd needed it. Until she needed it. Now they'd both gone back to living their lives. The End.

As far as endings went, it was a good one. His mind took him back to a sunny summer day at the zoo with the sweet smell of cotton candy in the air and the coppery tang of blood.

He hadn't died that day but he might as well have. Losing his children had left him dead inside. He'd never let himself look too closely at just why he'd brought his service weapon up to Mitch's cabin.

Now he was back where he belonged and Mallory was where she should be. Yeah, a good ending. Something kicked his heart at that thought. He put the beer to his lips and drank deeply to drown it.

A news program began. The anchor started the run down of the days events. First up was an appeal to the public for information on a woman who'd been abducted. A photo flashed on the screen. Mallory. Gage was off the stool and as close to the TV as he could get before he'd taken his next breath. The anchor identified Mallory in her official capacity as an FBI agent and added that she'd been taken from her home. The report ended with a clip of Mallory's superior, York, requesting that anyone with information should contact the Bureau. A telephone number scrolled along the bottom of the screen. The report was over almost as soon as it began, but in that brief time Gage's heart rate soared until he felt it would burst from his chest.

Considine. It had to be Considine. The bastard had her. Images popped into Gage's mind. Mallory being interrogated. Mallory bleeding and in pain. Mallory dead. Gage felt a tsunami of fear, fear he'd never known for himself. He raced for the exit.

Mallory's apartment would be his first stop. He needed to see where she'd been taken.

He made good time, but then he hadn't observed any speed limits, driving pedal to the metal the whole way, pushing the old truck regardless of how she quivered as the speedometer needle swung farther to the right.

At the apartment, he ignored the crime scene tape and went inside. His blood ran cold. The place was trashed. Mallory had not gone without a fight. The thought came to Gage that her abductors had needed to apply significant force to take her out of here.

The image of Mallory hurt returned to him, so strong now that he was actually faced with the reality of it. He wanted to storm Considine's home like an enraged bull. A desperate thought that wouldn't help her. He needed to keep his head. Breathing hard, he concentrated on doing just that and to force himself to think like a cop, not a man who … cared about her.

The crime scene team had been all over the apartment. Gage didn't know what he hoped to find. In the end he found nothing but blood. He honed on a patch of blood that had dried on the kitchen floor. He closed his eyes briefly, then turned away from it.

He went to see York next. York was moving about the office like a hurricane. Gage stepped into York's path, halting him. "Where do things stand with Billy Wilder?" Gage knew it was professional courtesy for a fellow cop that had York considering how to respond to the question rather than blowing Gage off outright.

"Wilder's dead," York said. "He died in lock up. I got the report from our people earlier today that he was murdered."

"Considine?"

"Investigation is ongoing, but he looks good for this."

A burn started in Gage's stomach. Considine was cleaning house and Mallory was next. "What about the women?"

"Wilder was our only lead." York clenched his fists. "We've started a canvass of the apartments and of the area. Someone had to have seen something."

Gage knew the drill. Knew that witness accounts were most often sketchy. Memories were faulty. Precious time could be wasted tracking down false clues. And all the while Mallory was in Considine's hands. Fear seized Gage again, and for an instant he couldn't move. He forced himself back from that edge, forced himself to shake off the fear and bring himself back to the moment.

He addressed York again. "Do you have anything else on Considine to bring him in and force him to give up Mallory?"

"Not a damn thing."

"Sir?"

A female agent reached them and addressed York. Gage left them to their conversation.

* * *

Mallory came awake slowly. Her first conscious thought was one of pain. Fighting waves of dizziness and nausea, she clasped her head as if to stop something in there from causing her this hurt. She took a breath. Agony shot through her side, threatening to send her back into the void of unconsciousness.

She closed her eyes and worked on taking shallow breaths. She didn't know where she was but she recalled the two men who'd broken into her apartment and abducted her.

She smelled mold and somewhere water dripped, striking a surface with a plop that echoed. Her hands and feet were free. If restraints hadn't been used then that meant her abductors were secure in the knowledge that she wouldn't be able to get away.

She opened her eyes again slowly against another level of pain. It was black as night and cold. Clutching her side, she raised herself from the floor, and braced herself against a wall at her back. The room spun. No doubt she was concussed. As she held her head in her hands she thought a concussion would be the least of her worries.

She heard squeaking. A rodent of some kind was in this space with her. Mallory shivered and huddled into herself at the thought of rats.

She squinted in the darkness and as her eyes adjusted, she made out small details. A large tank of some kind butted up against a wall. A staircase lay beyond that. And in the darkness beyond the stairs something moved. Something too big to be a mouse. Mallory swallowed a scream. She wasn't in here alone. Something else was in here with her.

* * *

Gage left the FBI building. Mitch's truck was

struggling. Gage didn't want to risk breaking down. He went back to the car rental agency, got an SUV, and left the old truck parked on the long-term lot next door. At a local electronics chain, he bought a cell phone and a laptop then checked into a hotel.

He didn't have the envelope he and Mallory had found in Wilder's locker. Either York or Considine had it now. But Gage and Mallory had been on the internet sites listed enough times for him to recall them. He logged onto where Mallory had posted profiles. If he could find the guy who was trolling these sites, he'd have a link to the traffickers. He went to all the sites. No one had made contact.

Billy Wilder was the only link they'd had to the traffickers and his death had effectively severed that link. He needed to find another one.

He logged onto the Washington PD data base. Two hours later, he'd gone over all the data gathered on Paul Considine. The man was scum and had ties to organized crime, but there was nothing to connect Considine with Billy Wilder.

Fuck. He was missing something.

Mallory's abductors had been instructed to take her to a mountain cabin when the accident occurred and she landed on Gage's doorstep. Billy Wilder's cabin, specifically. Could they be holding her there now?

The location to the cabin had been among the personal papers they'd found in Wilder's locker. Gage knew where the place was. He grabbed his coat and keys and charged out of the hotel room, praying that when he reached the cabin, he would find her and, find her alive.

He abandoned the vehicle a distance from the cabin and crept over the snow covered landscape. It was still afternoon and he kept to the trees and out of the sunlight where he would be exposed to anyone who happened to glance out of Billy's windows.

The cabin was small. No vehicles were parked in the vicinity. No smoke rose from the chimney. No foot prints in the snow led to the cabin's front door.

The place appeared unoccupied. Still, he moved closer. He wouldn't turn around until he'd made sure that Mallory wasn't being held inside.

He went around the back and found another entrance. Standing beneath an overhang, he used his flashlight to smash a window in that door, then went inside. Moving carefully, he blended into the shadows, making his way through each room of the cabin. It was as cold as a freezer, reinforcing Gage's impression that there wasn't anyone there. He finished searching the place. Mallory wasn't there.

* * *

Mallory fought back dizziness and got to her feet. She had to know what was in here with her. She braced to fight should she need to defend herself, the effort pathetic. But as she drew closer, she realized it was a person. A woman. No, not one woman, several women. Her breath caught. Twelve women.

Her pulse raced as she limped to them. As one,

they shrank back. One whimpered. Another wrapped her arms around her knees and made a low, keening sound. Their fear was palpable and Mallory's heart broke.

"Please don't be afraid of me." It hurt to talk and she was thirsty. Her voice cracked. She needed to do better than that if she was going to reassure them. She swallowed a couple of times. "My name is Mallory Burke. I'm a federal agent. I've been looking for you."

"You've been looking for us?"

The voice that came out of the darkness was weak and thin. Concern for the woman had Mallory increasing her pace as much as she was able. "Yes and I'm going to get all of you out of here, I promise you."

"But how? You're caught too."

"I will find a way. Please trust me."

The sound of footfalls drawing nearer drew her attention away from the women. The steps stopped at the top of the stairs. Someone was out there. An instant later the door swung wide.

A light appeared at the top of the stairs and a hulking figure filled the doorway. He stood in silhouette for an instant, back lit by a bare bulb in the ceiling, then a flashlight winked on and he began his descent. Some light filtered down and showed they were in a cellar. Mallory recognized the man on the stairs as the big brute from her apartment and felt a rush of anger. Automatic weapons were strapped to his chest. He held a tray laden with sandwiches and bottles of water. Mallory's stomach was roiling like a storm tossed sea from the pain in her head and from fear. She didn't think she'd keep food down, but she curled her fingers into her palm to keep from showing him how badly she wanted the water.

Big Brute reached Mallory and the other women. They huddled together trying to make themselves as small as possible. Again, Mallory assumed a fighting stance, drawing on her badly depleted physical resources, and placed herself between them and him.

He aimed the light in her eyes. She raised a hand to deflect the piercing glare and he laughed.

"How do you like your digs?" he said.

"Where is this place?"

"You don't need to be worrying about that."

"How long have I been here?"

"You're just full of questions aren't you? I might be willing to answer some of them for you." He stroked his chin as he looked her up and down. "What's it worth to you?"

Mallory tasted bile.

Another man appeared at the steps. The other man who'd helped Big Brute abduct her. Automatic weapons were strapped to his chest as well and she got the sinking sensation that these men were mercenaries.

"Hey, quit jabbering," Big Brute's partner said. "Give them the food then get back here. I need your help up here."

Big Brute plopped the tray onto the concrete floor. He leered at Mallory. "Later, when it's just you here, I'll be back."

"Just me?"

"These girls are going on a long boat ride in the morning. Hear that, girls. You're getting picked up from here in just about ten hours." He leaned toward Mallory and whispered, "Like I said, later."

A couple of the women were sobbing now. Mallory had promised to get them all out of here but how was she going to do that? She had no plan. And only until morning to come up with one.

* * *

Gage returned to the hotel after leaving Billy's cabin. He logged onto the dating sites again. He found nothing and his desperation mounted. He called York for an update on the search. York had nothing new to add. Gage longed for ten minutes alone with Considine.

Gage checked his watch. Again. Three minutes since the last time he'd looked. Twelve minutes since he'd checked the dating sites. The window in his hotel room overlooked a busy street. It was only six p.m., but dark due to the season and the streetlights glowed. People in coats with thick wool scarves wrapped around their faces hurried down the sidewalks, likely on their way home to dinner.

Gage didn't want to think of Mallory hurt and afraid, but he could think of nothing else. He clutched the window sill and leaned his brow against the wall, squeezing his eyes shut, riding out a fear for her that threatened to derail him.

He straightened away from the window for another check of the sites. Someone had left a response.

He scanned the message. The guy signed the email as "Neil". The tone of the note was light and friendly. Gage's heart raced. He recalled Kyle from the park. Could be nothing more than that—some pimply kid wanting a hook up. But even as he thought that, he was considering how to respond. He sent back a reply. Whoever had gotten in touch was online because a message appeared almost at once.

The exchange of emails went on for some time. Gage held himself in check, barely. He could not blow this. It may be his only lead to getting Mallory back.

At last, he received the message he'd been waiting for—a request to meet. He sat tense waiting for the location. It came in the form of an invitation to a house party at nine o'clock that evening. He replied with a yes, and an address was provided.

As he and Mallory had done with the meeting in the park, Gage arrived at the destination early. He parked one block away from the street, then hoofed it to the house.

The address belonged to a tidy bungalow that had been built around the time of the second world war. The house looked well maintained with a pink tricycle on a small porch. Could be camouflage but it gave him pause. Regardless, he pressed on, praying this wasn't another dead end.

He took up a position across the road from the house and away from the streetlights. There'd been no activity since he'd moved into this position. No guests arrived. No one left the house.

It was time for a closer look. He crossed the

street to the bungalow, listened for barking. Nothing. No dog then.

He scaled the fence around the property then circled the building, peering into the side and back windows. All were blocked with blinds until he came to a small window in the kitchen door. No loud music penetrated to the outside that would suggest a party was underway. He peered through the glass. No one was in the kitchen or in the portion of the hall he was able to see. But on the table were restraints and a syringe.

As he had at Billy's cabin, he used his flashlight and broke the window. Moving quickly in case anyone had heard the glass break, he let himself into the house. Footsteps padded on the stairs. A man came up from the basement. Thirty something with a diamond stud in one ear lobe and an Italian suit over his tall, toned frame.

Gage grabbed him by the neck.

The guy cried out. "What the fuck!"

"Are you Neil?"

"Yeah! Yeah!"

Gage slammed Neil into a wall. Blood spurted from Neil's now broken nose and flowed from his split lips. A photograph of a boat hung on that same wall. The picture shook then struck the floor, shattering the glass frame.

Gage kept Neil's face squashed against the plaster and stuck the barrel of the gun into his ear.

"Man, you don't know who you're messing with." Neil was lisping. He'd broken a tooth when his face hit the wall. "Hope you said your prayers last night. Cause you're about to meet your maker."

"That so?" Gage ground the gun into Neil's ear and received the satisfaction of hearing him shriek.

Panting from the pain, Neil yelled, "You are going to pray for death before I'm through with you!"

"Big talk. I'm not some young girl you can put a scare into."

Neil went still.

Gage sneered. "Yeah. You're finally getting it. I'm here about your invite to a house party here tonight."

"Man, I don't know what you're talking about."

"I have your emails setting this whole thing up, *man*. You're going down for this."

Damp circles appeared on Neil's fine suit and Gage smelled the rank odor of perspiration.

"I wasn't gonna do nothing to that chick tonight," Neil said.

"I saw the restraints and the syringe."

"How much you want? I got money. Name your price." Neil's words came out in a rush.

"Where is Agent Mallory Burke?"

"What? Who?"

Gage jammed the gun deeper into Neil's ear. His knees buckled and he whimpered.

"I don't know!" he screamed. "I don't know anything about any Agent Burke! I just get the girls for him! That's all! I swear!"

It was clear Neil didn't know anything about Mallory. "Who do you get the girls for?"

"He'll kill me, man, if I tell you."

His voice harsh and deadly, Gage said, "What do I think I'm going to do to you if you don't?"

"Okay! Okay! It's Manning! It's Manning!"

Gage frowned. "Congressman Manning?"

"Yeah. I told you what you want to know. Now let me go. I gotta leave town. Leave the country or I'm a dead man."

"Where's Manning?"

"I don't know, man, I don't know!"

Gage rammed Neil's head into the wall again. Neil's eyes rolled white. Gage released him and Neil crumpled at Gage's feet.

Manning. Gage recalled Billy Wilder's notation on the backs of the photographs—the letters p.m. Pritchard Manning? He'd spearheaded the trafficking investigation and executed a perfect shell game. With the feds focused on Considine, it was business as usual for Manning.

As Gage took that in, he pulled out his cell phone. York would be the one to call. He had the full resources of the feds and would be able to act quickly on this information. But York was Manning's FBI contact. Could he trust York or was York working with Manning? Gage didn't know and until he did, he was on his own.

CHAPTER TWELVE

Gage put Neil in the basement, cuffed to a support beam with his own restraints. He'd be taken into custody once Mallory was safe. Tracking Congressman Manning had been ridiculously easy. The congressman was at a hotel in Manhattan, attending a campaign fundraiser being held in his honor.

Gage joined the guests dressed in their finery in the lavish ballroom. Manning was at the podium. Gage had to fight back a rage to pull Manning off that stage and pound him into the floor.

Gage stepped onto the red carpet that covered the center aisle of the grand room and approached the podium. "Tell me, Congressman," he called out, "how is the investigation into the human trafficking operation progressing?"

Manning drew back. Gage saw recognition in his eyes. Not surprising since Manning had been observing Mallory that he knew who Gage was. *Game on.*

Manning recovered his aplomb. The others in the room had no knowledge of the charade being played out before them. No doubt to maintain appearances to these constituents Manning said, "Unfortunately, there have been no new developments in the investigation."

"Not since the murder of Billy Wilder."

The congressman pressed his lips together hard enough that the corners of his mouth went white. "I'm not at liberty to divulge details of an ongoing investigation. If you're here for the press conference, you're one day early. Come back tomorrow and I'll be happy to answer your questions."

I bet you will. Gage continued to close the distance between them. He trained his gaze on Manning, eyeing the congressman as if he had him in his cross hairs. This man who had Mallory.

"What is being done about the disappearance of Agent Burke, taken by this so-called, self-proclaimed 'Don'."

Manning's eyes bulged and his face reddened with barely contained anger. He appeared incapable of speech and when he finally did speak, his voice shook with rage. "We're all praying for the safe return of Agent Burke. Again, I'm not at liberty to discuss the investigation. You're delaying these proceedings. If you don't leave, I'll be forced to call for security."

Gage was directly in front of the stage now. He pitched his voice low so only Manning could hear, his tone harsh and lethal. "That's too bad.

Then I'll have to tell them what you'll want to keep between us. Now, get off the stage. Unless you want me to tell everyone in here what I know about the leader of the trafficking ring."

Manning seized the microphone in a white-knuckled grip. "Ladies and gentlemen, please excuse me for a few moments."

Gage jutted his thumb for the congressman to precede him into the hotel lobby. Two of Manning's bodyguards strode toward them. The congressman sent them back with a quick swipe of his hand.

"You put on quite a show to get my attention, Broderick." Though Manning's voice was low, there was no mistaking his anger. "I hope your little dog and pony act was worth it."

"I know you're behind the trafficking operation not Considine."

Manning didn't bother to deny it. "If you could prove that we wouldn't be having this conversation. You bore me." He shot his cuffs and straightened diamond studded cuff links. "I have people waiting." He turned away.

"Whether or not I can prove it in a court of law is irrelevant. I don't plan to go to the Feds with what I know."

"Money?" He threw back his head and laughed. "You think to extort money? From me? Are you nothing more than an opportunist?" Gage maintained eye contact and a silence. "Not money, then." Manning scoffed. "If you defame my character, I promise you will regret it."

Gage eyed Manning. "I'm going to Considine."

Manning's lips quivered. He paled and a fine sheen of sweat coated his face.

Gage's voice harsh and lethal he said, "Considine is not going to care about bringing you to federal justice. You're running a human trafficking ring in what he considers his territory. He's going to put you in the ground somewhere. For that, and for all the heat you brought to bear on him with your so-called task force. And that's after he's taken you apart piece by piece."

At his sides, Manning's hands balled into fists. Gage believed if the congressman thought he stood a chance, he would pounce on Gage. *Go for it.*

But Manning wasn't that brave or that stupid to take Gage on.

"What do you want?" Manning said.

"You and I are going on a road trip."

Only to avoid attracting attention, did Gage quell the urge to seize the congressman by the throat and propel him to the exit.

Gage led Manning to the SUV, parked across the street from the hotel. When they were both inside the vehicle, he turned to the congressman. "Where is Mallory?"

"All this because of her?"

"Where is she?"

Manning gave Gage a venomous look. "I also have a cabin in those mountains."

They made the drive in silence other than when necessary for Manning to provide directions. Once Gage was on the mountain's access road, he no longer needed Manning to guide him. Despite the distance, he could see the cabin, bathed in the glow of a full moon. It was an impressive structure. Built near the edge of the mountain, the view of the snow-capped landscape below was spectacular.

Gage stopped the SUV on the access road. He wanted to drive up to the front door of the cabin. Fuck, he wanted to drive right into the cabin and get Mallory, but the snow in front was too deep for the vehicle.

Here was where things got tricky. Where Gage could be overpowered. He took out his gun and aimed at Manning. "Call the cabin. Put your phone on speaker. Tell them to bring Agent Burke out."

"What about me?"

"Make the call."

Manning did as Gage instructed. "This is the Don."

"Yes, sir."

"I want you to bring Agent Burke out to the porch."

"Sir, did I hear you right? You want me to take her outside?"

"Do it. Now."

As Manning gave the order, Gage closed his eyes briefly in relief. She was alive.

Gage kept his gun trained on Manning and divided his gaze between Manning and the cabin's front door. The temperature was near freezing but sweat broke out on his brow.

A light came on outside. The door opened. A burly man stepped onto the porch. An automatic weapon hung from a shoulder strap and an arsenal was strapped to his chest. Two more men, both as heavily armed as the first, exited the cabin. Mallory came out last. Gage wanted to go to her, but held himself back.

He lowered the truck's windows and put the gun to Manning's head. "Tell them to ask Agent Burke to come to the truck. She comes alone. They wait on the porch."

The congressman stuck his head out the window and relayed the order. The man who'd brought Mallory outside replied that she was injured. She wouldn't be able to get to the vehicle on her own and Gage was forced to give the go ahead for her to be escorted.

Gage watched without blinking as Mallory staggered off the porch. She was leaning heavily on the man with her and Gage's stomach clenched that she was hurt so badly, she was unable to walk unaided. His hand tightened on the grip of the gun he held on Manning, but he put the fear and rage that bubbled up inside him aside for the moment and focused on her halting progress. *Come on, baby*.

When Mallory and her escort were about half way between the porch and the SUV she struck the man and broke free. Her fingers closed around the automatic but her captor broke her grip. He snagged a fistful of her hair. Her head snapped back and she cried out with pain.

Gage saw red and was out of the SUV intent on doing grave bodily harm to the one who'd hurt her when Mallory managed to break free again. "Mallory!"

She turned to him and her eyes went wide. She mouthed his name. His throat tightened.

Gage still had the gun locked on the congressman. He glanced away from Mallory to Manning then back to Mallory. "Come to me. We're getting out of here."

As she started toward him, it was all he could do not to carry her out of there. But he forced himself to hold his ground and keep his gun trained on Manning.

She stepped into the beam from the SUV's headlights. A few feet from Gage, her step faltered and her knees buckled. He moved then, and caught her against him, preventing her from landing face down in the snow. In that instant, Manning bolted out of the truck, taking cover below the passenger door.

"I'm out!" Manning shouted. Stop them! Don't let them get away!"

Gage had just lost his leverage. He swept Mallory up in his arms.

She clung to him. "Gage! The women are here!"

He set her down on the front seat. "We'll get them."

He'd find a place to secure Mallory first, then come back for the women on his own. He gave Mallory a nudge and she crawled over the console. As she reached the passenger side, the man who'd led her from the porch reached in and hauled her out. Mallory landed a hit to the man's face but he stood her against his body and pressed the barrel of a gun to her head.

"Drop your weapon, Broderick, and put your hands behind your head," Manning shouted. "Or my man will drop her."

To drive home Manning's words, the man who held Mallory ground the gun against her temple. She bit her lip in an attempt to keep from crying out, Gage thought, but he didn't need the added inducement. From the instant the man had Mallory, Gage's course of action was set. He would not risk her life. He let his gun fall to the snow and linked his fingers behind his head.

Manning waved a hand at the two men on the porch and they ran toward him. The congressman was a tall, imposing man, but between the two other men he looked like a small child. Bolstered by his bodyguards he went to stand in front of Gage. His lip curled in a sneer and the look in his eyes was of pure malice.

"You dared to put your hands on me." Manning's eyes glittered with hatred. He turned to one of the giants beside him and nodded.

The man drove his ham-sized fist into Gage's gut. Mallory screamed. Gage's breath whooshed out. On the heels of that blow, another connected with Gage's face. He staggered but glared at the man who'd hit him and remained on his feet.

Mallory screamed again. "No!"

If not for the gun to Mallory's head, Gage would have given as well as he got, but his hands were tied, figuratively, if not literally, and everyone there knew that.

A third blow landed again on Gage's face and this time he dropped to one knee. Eyeing Manning, he spat blood on the congressman's polished shoe.

Manning's face and neck turned crimson. A vein on his brow began to pulse. "Wrap this up. I need to get back to my party."

Two blows hit Gage in rapid succession, then a third powerful hit struck the side of his head. Gage fell forward. He never knew when his face landed in the snow.

* * *

One of Manning's men lifted Gage's unconscious body from the snow and hoisted him over his shoulder. Gage didn't even groan and Mallory's heart lurched.

With one heavy hand on her shoulder and another squeezing her arm, Big Brute marched Mallory back to the cellar. Gage was dumped on the concrete floor.

Mallory kneeled beside him. Patting his cheeks, she called out his name, but he didn't respond. She didn't know what good being conscious would do him at the moment. No doubt he was better off not being awake to feel the pain of the beating he'd sustained. It was a purely selfish move on her part that she wanted him awake.

She wanted his head, at least, off the cold, damp floor. She sat against the wall and ignoring her own hurts, put her hands under his shoulders to lift him onto her lap. She heaved, but he was too heavy and fell back. She tried again with the same result.

"Let me help you."

In the darkness, Mallory could not make out the features of the woman who came forward. She crouched beside Gage and added her strength to

Mallory's. Between the two of them, they lifted him.

"Thank you," Mallory said.

"Who is he?"

The woman had a soft Caribbean accent.

"He's—" *The man I love.* Mallory held the words back and said instead, "Police Captain Gage Broderick. We've been working together to find all of you."

"It's been so long since I was caught, I thought no one was still looking. That no one cared."

Mallory clasped the other woman's hand. "We care. What is your name?"

"Lucinda."

"How long ago were you abducted, Lucinda?"

"I've lost count of the weeks."

It sounded like Lucinda was among the first taken for this latest shipment and Manning had been keeping her while he took the necessary time to capture the others. "How did it happen?"

"I was on my way home from school. I attend evening classes at the university. I was studying to be a nurse." Her voice broke. "A man asked me for the time. That was all. I looked to my watch and I don't know what happened after that. When I woke up, I was in a moving vehicle." Her voice trailed off.

One by one, the other women came forward and told their stories. Mallory's heart wrenched as she listened but also, her anger built that these women had been torn from their lives at the whim of one man. Her anger built, and her resolve to see them home safely.

Gage groaned. "Mallory?"

She put her hand on his cheek. "I'm here. How are you feeling?"

"I'll live." He grunted. "Where are we?"

"Manning's cabin. In the cellar. Not Considine." She shook her head. "It's been Manning all along. Now that I know that, it's no mystery how my cover was blown."

"Yeah. He covered his tracks." Gage's muscles tensed. "Who's in here with us?"

"The women we've been looking for."

"I am Lucinda, Captain Broderick."

Gage turned his head in the direction of the voice coming out of the darkness. The others spoke their names. Their spirits had been battered but not broken.

"Ladies," Gage said.

He raised his head from Mallory's lap, groaned again, but didn't lay back down. He turned to his side, went still for a moment, then braced his arms on the cement and pushed himself up off the floor.

"Easy." Mallory put her hands on his shoulders in an attempt to steady him "Take it slow." She kept her hands on him until he sat back against the wall. "How did you find me?"

"We got a hit on one of your profiles. You were right about those dating sites."

He filled in the details for her. Mallory told him what went down at her apartment on the day she was brought here.

"How badly did they hurt you?" Gage's voice was low and harsh with concern.

"Not as badly as they hurt you." She shook her head, though he couldn't see that. "I'm so sorry,

Gage."

"For what?"

"If I had kept my feet under me, we would all have been long away from here."

"Not your fault. That son of a bitch hurt you." His voice was hard. "Will you be able to walk out of here?"

"This time I'll do what needs doing."

Gage raised his voice, "Ladies, are any of you hurt?"

All responded that they were not which made sense since Manning would not want them damaged for the sale.

"Manning is transporting the women in a few hours," Mallory said.

Gage was silent for a moment then said, "I counted three men when we were outside. Are there more?"

"None that I saw. Gage, they're mercenaries. They know how to fight and aren't afraid to."

"Yeah, and they'll fight to the death since defeat would mean their death anyway. Were you conscious to see the cellar in the light?"

"Yes."

"Where are the exits?"

"There's only one," Mallory said. "The door at the top of the stairs."

"Okay. Then that's going to have to be it. A few hours you said?"

"Yes."

Gage addressed the women again. "Ladies, we're getting out of here. When they come for you, we'll make our move."

* * *

Gage had been in tenuous situations in his years on the job. He'd known fear, certainly, but never the kind of fear that he was feeling now. They'd heard footsteps outside the cellar door a moment ago. The hour to transport the women was at hand. It was time they all got out of there.

The lives of the women Manning planned to sell depended on what he did in the next moments. Mallory's life depended on it. A moment from his past flashed across his mind. Another setting. Another circumstance. Two precious others who'd depended on him.

And he'd failed.

He was scared shitless of failing again. Battling a fear for Mallory that threatened to paralyze him. If anything went wrong, if he went wrong, Manning would kill her and do so with relish.

There were three mercenaries that he knew of at the cabin. All with enough firepower to blow this place and everyone in it into the next millennium.

The footsteps stopped. Gage got into position. He braced. The door opened and the man Mallory had named Big Brute stepped onto the landing. Gage raised his arm. He chopped the hulk on the back of the neck. Big Brute crumpled in on himself and fell in a heap at Gage's feet. He disarmed the mercenary, then secured him to the metal railing with a pair of handcuffs he found on the man's belt.

Mallory joined him on the stairs and took one of Big Brute's hand guns for herself. The women crowded on the stairs behind her. Mallory had told him of a rear exit in the cabin and would now lead the women to safety while he stayed back and took out the remaining mercenaries. The keys to the SUV had been left in the ignition when Gage was caught. He'd told her where the vehicle was parked, but they'd decided she'd drive the women out in whatever vehicle Manning had sent for their transport if possible, in case the keys were no longer there or the SUV had been disabled.

With a nod to Mallory, Gage led them out of the cellar. They moved in silence. He was hoping to get them safely away then make his own way out without firing one round. Once gun fire erupted, the mercenaries he knew about and any more Manning had sent for the transport would come on the run.

He peered around a corner, checking the hall that held the rear door. It was clear. He kept his gaze and the automatic weapon trained, keeping himself between Mallory and the other women as they made their way down the corridor. A couple of other rooms branched off this hall. The women had to pass by them on their way to the exit and his shoulders tensed as he envisioned one of the mercs leaping out at them. No doubt Manning's men were under orders not to hurt the twelve women and compromise the sale, but they would have no such compunction when it came to Mallory.

The women were almost to the door when Gage heard laughter. One of the mercenaries entered the hall. His gaze locked on Gage and his brows arched in surprise. He went for his gun. Gage opened fire.

"Go!" He shouted to Mallory.

* * *

Mallory watched one of the mercenaries fall. Another came running. Her stomach knotted. There were more than three of them here now. Gage let loose with the automatic, and the man leaped back and took cover behind a wall. Gage fired another few rounds. Mallory knew he wanted to bring anyone else in the cabin to him. He would keep Manning's men pinned down and focused on him so she and the women could make their escape.

The cat was out of the bag as far as their escape went and with no further reason for stealth, Mallory and the women ran out the door. She needed to see the women to safety, but she could not leave Gage to fight off an untold number of mercenaries indefinitely by himself. As good as he was, he was just one man and eventually they would overpower him and he would be killed. Her heart stuttered and a cold fear coursed through her.

Outside, the sky was pink with early morning. The cold penetrated to the bones. Mallory wore only the blouse and skirt she'd worn to work on the day she was taken from her apartment and the other women were similarly dressed. As they made their way from the cabin in knee deep snow, they shivered.

They reached the front of the cabin. A luxury

sedan was parked on the access road, beside Gage's rented SUV and behind that, a van. The engine of the van was running. A plume of smoke from the rear tail pipe rose into the air. No one was behind the steering wheel. They appeared to be alone on the road. Still, when the women would have raced to the vehicle, Mallory held them back. When she was sure they were alone, she led the way to the van, threw open the rear doors and the women climbed in.

As Lucinda was about to join the other women in the back, Mallory caught her by the arm. "Can you drive?"

Lucinda nodded.

"Then drive out of here. Straight ahead. You'll come to a main road that will take you into town. Call York at the FBI office in Bradley. Tell him everything."

Lucinda blinked quickly. "What about you?"

Another barrage of gunfire shattered the quiet.

"I'll be fine." Mallory squeezed Lucinda's fingers in a desperate plea. "Please. Just go now."

Lucinda nodded, then got behind the steering wheel and floored the accelerator. The van disappeared down the mountain.

The gunfire stopped. In the near-absolute quiet, Mallory heard a block of ice fall from the roof.

Gage.

She whirled and ran back to the cabin. Five men lay on the floor and one of them was Gage. Mallory dropped to her knees beside him. "Gage!"

Blood coated one side of his head. She felt as if her heart stopped. She dropped her gun on the floor and took his face between her palms. "Gage!" But he was alive. She could feel his pulse beating beneath her fingers.

"Remarkable. He killed all of my men before dying himself."

Manning's voice came from behind Mallory. He drew back his foot and kicked her gun across the room.

Mallory's pulse pounded and she rose to her feet slowly to put herself between Manning and Gage so the congressman wouldn't see that Gage was alive. She needed to get Manning away from Gage and where an instant earlier she prayed for him to open his eyes, now she prayed for him to keep them closed until she'd led the congressman away. To that end, she began inching to the exit.

Manning stalked her. "You've led me on a merry chase, but that's over now." He closed the distance between them and seized her by the throat. He pressed the barrel of the gun to the back of her neck and shoved her the rest of the way to the door.

He pushed her outside, to the back of the cabin where the view of the mountains stretched out before them. The mountains rose against a clear blue sky. Sunlight glinted off the pristine snow.

"Breathtaking isn't it?" Manning said. "This mountain attests to the presence of a higher power. Man has attempted to imitate but has never been able to recreate such perfection. I'm going to have to leave here and not return. It saddens me to think I will never see this again." His tone was wistful, then became menacing. "I owe you for that as well, Agent Burke."

She knew she shouldn't rile him but she couldn't hold the words back. "You are a monster. You deserve everything the justice system can do to you."

He laughed. "Can you still believe in our system? All the while I've held an exalted position with our government, I've been building my own private empire. Twenty years, Agent Burke. My, where has the time gone."

Twenty years. Since before Cassie's abduction. The impact hit Mallory. Was it possible Manning was also responsible for Cassie? If he hadn't kept records they would never have proof, but by his own admission it was probable.

Hatred like she'd never known rose within Mallory. "You'll have time to ponder that question while you're on death row. Though there hasn't been an execution in years, in case you've forgotten, Congressman, New York is still a death penalty state."

His smile slipped. The color drained from his cheeks. "I'm going to enjoy dropping you off my mountain."

Mallory braced, seeking a chance to disarm Manning but his grip on her remained tight and the gun remained pressed hard to her nape.

She fought back nerves as he backed her to the edge of the mountain. She tried to dig in and hold her ground, but couldn't keep a foothold in the snow. When they reached the edge, Manning delighted in dangling her weak leg over the cliff.

"Let her go, Manning."

It was Gage. He was holding a semi-automatic trained on Manning but the congressman's grip on her meant Gage couldn't shoot Manning without Mallory going over the edge as well.

Manning gasped in surprise then swung around, bringing Mallory to stand beside him. "I don't believe I'll do that."

Manning tightened his hold on her throat and Mallory gagged. Though Gage's grip on the gun was rock-steady, she saw sweat bead on his brow.

"She's no good to you dead," Gage said.

"Or to you," Manning responded. "Looks like we're at a standoff."

Manning smiled and gave her a little push so that she teetered on the edge of the cliff. It was only the congressman's hold on her that kept her from falling. Whereas before she wanted nothing more than for him to release her, now, she seized his arms with both hands, hanging on for her life.

She was shivering from the cold and from fear. The wind picked up and she feared that the slight increase to the breeze might be enough to unbalance her and send her over the edge.

She saw her own fear mirrored in Gage's eyes and knew he was going to put down his gun. Manning would kill him and her too. She scrambled for a way to save them both but her mind went blank.

The whup whup of helicopter blades cut the air and the marking on the chopper identified it as government issue. Lucinda and the women must have reached safety and had sent help.

The helicopter hovered above them. The door opened. A man crouched in the opening with a rifle aimed at them.

Someone on the helicopter spoke through a

loud speaker: "Drop your weapon and back away from the woman!"

"No!"

Gage shouted the command at the chopper, then addressed the congressman. "Manning you can still walk away from this." Gage's voice vibrated with emotion.

Manning smiled. Horror filled Gage's eyes. Manning continued to watch Gage as he stepped back off the mountain, taking Mallory with him.

Mallory screamed. Gage lunged. He caught her hand in one of his and his fingers clamped around her.

"Gage!"

He dropped onto his belly. She reached up and grasped his wrist with both of her hands while he brought his other hand around and grabbed her by the elbow.

Manning was still holding on to her, now by one foot. Clearly, he wanted to make sure she died with him.

Gage's gun was in the snow beside him within easy reach to shoot Manning but he would need to take one hand off Mallory to do that, and he couldn't keep her from falling down the rest of the mountain with just one hand.

His arms trembled with the strain of so much weight. His face reddened and the veins in his neck bulged.

He would not be able to pull them both up. She kicked back, striking the congressman in the face. Still, he held on. Her hand slipped in Gage's and she dropped a little further down the mountain. She screamed. Gage slid forward. Now he was hanging over the edge, too.

He was not going to release her. If she didn't break Manning's hold, Gage would go down this mountain with them.

She brought her legs up then reared back, hitting Manning with all she was capable of. The congressman lost his grip on her. His screams echoed as he fell.

Gage reached down, seized her under one arm and pulled her up the mountain. Her teeth were chattering. She was trembling. He was shaking as well as he crushed her against him.

"I have you. I have you." He repeated the words over and over.

Dimly, Mallory realized that the helicopter had landed and men were running toward them. Tears filled her eyes. She buried her face in Gage's shoulder and let them come.

CHAPTER THIRTEEN

Mallory had the television in her apartment at low volume while she read a dossier on a new investigation. The cooking show she'd been listening to with half an ear as she skimmed background information ended and a talk show began. The host led with the story of Congressman Pritchard Manning who had been leading a double life as a respected politician and the head of a human trafficking operation. Shock waves of his secret criminal persona were rippling across the nation, the host said. Manning's picture appeared on the screen. Mallory picked up the remote and turned the television off.

It was five days since Manning stepped off that mountain and took her with him. She still got cold and shaky whenever she recalled that moment. She wrapped her arms around herself now and moved to the window. The snow storm that had precipitated her escape into the mountains had marked the end of the winter.

Spring had come early. Eight floors below, Bradley's residents were enjoying the mild afternoon. Mallory raised her face to the bright, warm sunlight.

Mallory's brother, John, came up beside her and put his arm around her. His dark hair was mussed as if he'd recently driven his fingers through it. When news broke about Manning and Mallory's role in apprehending the congressman, John had taken an emergency leave from his CIA team. Her brother was having a difficult time dealing with her near-death experience with Manning and since his arrival at her apartment, had taken to keeping her in his sights. John brought her close now and planted a kiss on the top of her head, then they just stood together, without speaking.

John's first night there, they'd stayed up until the early hours of the morning, talking about Manning and the investigation and about ... Cassie. There was little Mallory had never shared with John, and while he knew some of her driving need to find out what happened to Cassie, he hadn't known just how deep that need went. John had held her and rocked her as she'd told him of it, and cried for her dearest friend.

Footsteps behind them drew their attention. Mallory turned with John to see Eve, the woman John would marry at Christmas, coming toward them. Eve was bearing a tray with steaming mugs and a plate piled high with sandwiches.

"Thought you might like some lunch," Eve said as she set the tray down on the coffee table.

Eve smoothed her slim designer skirt beneath

her before gracefully lowering herself onto the armchair. John's eyes went soft and warm as he took in the woman he so clearly loved. Eve was a beautiful woman both outside and inside and Mallory welcomed her as a sister. Though she couldn't be happier that John and Eve had found each other, seeing them together also brought a degree of pain and a deep longing for Gage.

Like Mallory, Gage had given statements to York and to a bevy of high ranking government officials, and no doubt to his own police commissioner. But she hadn't heard that from him. She hadn't seen or spoken with Gage since he'd pulled her up that mountain.

Though it hurt to admit, she didn't expect to hear from him. They'd said all they needed to say outside the Bureau building on the day he left. Or, he had. After he'd spoken, there'd been nothing she could say. She was not over him and had accepted she never would be.

"Lunch sounds great, honey," John said to Eve. He faced Mallory. "How about it, Mal?"

Mallory left the window and accompanied her brother to the couch, welcoming the distraction from thinking about Gage. She hadn't told John or Eve about her love for Gage. The wound was too raw.

Eve bit delicately into an egg salad sandwich. "Mallory, I was hoping you and I could take a look at some bridal magazines after lunch."

Mallory swallowed a lump that formed in her throat and nodded. "Yes. Absolutely."

The doorbell rang. Mallory rose from the couch. She swung the front door open and went still at the sight of Gage standing in the corridor.

She took in a quick breath at the deep wound at his hairline that was healing but was still red and raw. He was wearing a dark suit and tie. It was the first time she'd seen him in anything but jeans and the business look had been made with him in mind. She hadn't thought he could possibly be more handsome, but he was.

"Hello, Mallory."

"Gage."

A silence dragged on. He broke it. "May I come in?"

She would have preferred not to invite him in. Seeing him had started her heart racing and had brought to the forefront every feeling she had for him. But after all they'd been through together, he certainly deserved better than to be left standing outside in the hall and she stepped back from the doorway.

John stood. Mallory cleared her throat to make introductions. "Gage, this is my brother, John, and his fiancée, Eve Collins. John, this is Gage Broderick."

John met Gage at the door and extended his hand. "Thank you."

Gage shook John's hand. "No thanks necessary."

Eve joined them. She cast a look to Gage and then to Mallory, then retrieved her coat and John's from the hall closet. "John, let's take a walk."

Before John or Mallory herself could utter a word, Eve hustled John out the door. Now alone with Gage, the silence resumed.

Gage looked around. "You changed some things."

"I replaced what was broken when Manning's men came in here."

"Looks good."

Mallory closed the door but kept her hand on the knob, needing something to hold on to. "I heard you were required to return to Washington."

"My boss, among others, wanted to know how I was involved in what went down over here."

"How'd that go?"

"I'm back to work."

Mallory felt happy for him. "I'm glad. You're a good cop. How does it feel being back?"

"Right." He gave her a level look. "How are you?"

"I'm fine, thank you. How are you?"

Gage's eyes narrowed on her, assessing her. "Really, how are you?"

After Gage pulled her up the mountain, she'd been treated for the ribs Big Brute had broken and the concussion he and his associate had caused, but to Gage now she said, "Really, I'm fine."

She couldn't do this with him. Couldn't stand here making small talk. Seeing him was one more assault to the delicate balance of her emotions. She felt her composure slip and turned the knob to open the door before she lost it completely.

"Mallory, we need to talk about how we left things."

She didn't want to hear reasons why they couldn't be together. Her heart breaking all over again, she said, "Gage, I don't want you to blame yourself for leaving the day that Manning got me. That wasn't your fault. You have nothing to feel guilty about." That guilt would have taken him over the mountain with her.

"Please. Hear me out."

She didn't want to do that. Not when his words were sure to pour salt on her bleeding heart. But he wasn't going to let this go and she was now dangerously close to breaking down. That would only upset them both. So before she did, she would let him get it all out and then he would leave her for the last time. Swallowing tears, she nodded

"When Ben and Josh were killed, something inside me died too," Gage said. "I went up to that mountain never expecting to come down."

Mallory rubbed the heel of her hand to her heart where it now ached for Gage.

He closed his eyes briefly. When he opened them, he went to the new bookcase in her living room where among tomes on investigative procedure and recent bestsellers, were photographs of Mallory at various ages with her parents, brothers, and Cassie. He stood facing them, but Mallory didn't think he was actually seeing the pictures.

"Up there," Gage continued, "I was in a place where no one could ever be hurt again because of me. Where I couldn't be hurt. I'd lost the two people I'd loved most in this world. I didn't want to love anyone again."

Mallory closed her eyes against the pain of those words. When she opened them, Gage had turned away from the photographs, back to her.

KAREN FENECH

"As long as I live I will never get the sight of you hanging off that mountain out of my head." Gage shuddered.

"You saved me. I'd be dead now if not for you."

"If I could remove the hurt that Manning caused you, and all the hurt I caused you ... " He shook his head. "I can't—"

Her heart squeezed. "I know you can't—" *Love me,* "—change how you feel."

"Change what happened."

"You don't have to do this, Gage. You have nothing to blame yourself for."

He left the bookcase and came to stand in front of her again. The expression on his face was raw and open, unlike any she'd seen on him before. "You think because I'd left you and then Manning caught you, I came after you out of guilt." His eyes blazed into hers. "Nothing I ever did with you was out of guilt."

Mallory just stared at him.

He framed her face between his broad palms. "I came after you because I love you."

Mallory's lips began to tremble. Her eyes stung with tears. Gage kissed her as the first one fell.

Against her lips he said, "I can't change what's happened, but I don't have to let that be all there is for us. I want a life with you." His voice was thick with emotion.

Mallory couldn't blink fast enough to clear the tears blurring her view of him. Kissing him, she murmured. "I want that too. I love you so much."

With Gage in Washington and her in New York, theirs would be a long distance relationship until they could get some things worked out, but for now all she could think was he was here holding her in his arms. "When do you need to go back home?"

Gage drew back from her. His gaze lit on each feature of her face before returning to meet her eyes. As his mouth covered hers again he said, "Baby, I am home."

TURN THE PAGE FOR A SPECIAL
PREVIEW OF KAREN FENECH'S NEXT
PROTECTORS NOVEL

PURSUED

Coming To Paperback Soon
Available Now As An eBook

PURSUED: The Protectors Series — Book Three

Chief Of Police Mitch Turner is finally close to getting the evidence he needs to prosecute crime boss, Christopher Rossington. When Mitch's fiancée, Shelby, is attacked, he must consider the attack wasn't random, but Rossington's attempt to strike out at Mitch. Shelby insists she wasn't targeted but Mitch has questions—about the attack and now about her ...

Dr. Shelby Grant appears to be living a fairytale life. She is doing meaningful work at her psychology practice and she's engaged to marry Mitch, the man of her dreams. But all is not as it appears. Nothing Mitch knows about her is the truth. She's been lying to him since the day they met and keeping a secret from him. She lives in fear he will find out what she is hiding. Her secret, if revealed, will destroy his love for her and will kill them both.

CHAPTER ONE

He was waiting for her outside the clinic. Shelby had no sooner stepped off the crumbling stoop of the faded, pre-second world war building and into the murky light of the one working street lamp when a man grabbed her from behind. She dropped her purse and briefcase onto the sidewalk that was littered with rotting garbage.

She managed a startled shriek before he hooked her at the neck, cutting off her voice and his arm clamped around her waist, crushing her against his body.

Shelby clawed at her attacker's arm. The man wore a light overcoat in deference to the nip in the air on the August night and her attempt to dig her nails into him was futile. She kicked back, striking him in the knee with the heel of her dress pump. He hissed in pain then his grip tightened, squeezing her wind pipe like a vise. She'd thought she couldn't breathe before, but now she couldn't take in any air at all.

No ... No!

In her mind she shouted that to him, but in reality she wasn't capable of making any sound other than desperate gasps for air.

Her attacker began dragging her down the sidewalk. She dug her heels into the cracked cement in an attempt to slow him down, but he was stronger and the dim light faded as they left the short street and entered the alley behind the clinic.

"Got a message for you," the man said.

Shelby froze as a new and entirely different fear rose within her.

He brought his lips to her ear. "Tick. Tock."

She didn't need to ask who the message was from. Her insides quivered. She whimpered.

"Hey! You, there! What you doin' to that woman?"

Shelby knew that voice. It was Joseph, the elderly maintenance man from the clinic. Her stomach tightened in fear for Joseph now as well as for herself. Any man sent to deliver this message would be ruthless and would have no qualms about killing Joseph. But, to Shelby's relief, the man who held her must not have perceived Joseph as a concern. He didn't even spare Joseph a glance. Message delivered, he released her. All of Shelby's weight had been balanced on him and she fell onto her hands and knees on the stained and broken asphalt. He stepped over her and strolled out of the alley.

"Lady! Lady! You all right?"

Joseph again. Shelby coughed and struggled to get up but couldn't manage to do so. Then Joseph was there in the alley with her. His face, worn and creased like old leather, bent to hers.

"It's you, Dr. Grant! Dr. Grant are you hurt?" Without waiting for a response, Joseph pulled a cell phone from the shirt pocket of his blue uniform. "I'm calling for an ambulance. You hold on, Dr. Grant."

* * *

Chief Of Police Mitchell Turner took the next turn, taking him onto the interstate leading out of Blake County, New York. Cars sped by his SUV making a soft whooshing sound. His police radio was tuned low though he could still make out the nasal voice of the woman working dispatch tonight.

Mitch cast another glance at his rearview. A late model sedan and a compact were still behind him where they'd been since he'd taken the on-ramp and pulled out in front of them. No other vehicles had followed him onto the highway.

Ten minutes later he was still in the clear and turned onto the deserted stretch of road that would take him to his destination. Trees lined both sides of what passed for this road and rose high into the sky but moonlight filtered through the branches, lighting his path. Gravel crunched beneath his tires, making a silent approach impossible if he'd wanted one. He didn't. He wanted the man he was meeting, Dan Harwick, to know he was on his way.

Harwick was working undercover, investigating Christopher Rossington whose business dealings were a front for organized crime. On the phone earlier today, Harwick sounded ... tense. A first for the cool-under-fire Harwick. Another first for Harwick was this request for an unscheduled meeting tonight. Mitch had never known Harwick to alter a plan and it concerned him.

Harwick had told Mitch he'd be driving a pickup truck for the meet. Mitch's headlights illuminated a truck parked at the edge of the road and Mitch was glad to see Harwick inside the vehicle. Harwick's cheeks hollowed as he drew deeply on a cigarette and the tip of the smoke glowed red. Mitch flicked the high beams as they'd agreed and pulled up alongside the truck.

Without preamble, Harwick said, "We got trouble, Mitch."

"Tell me."

Harwick met Mitch's gaze. "Rossington's got a mole in our investigation."

Mitch had taken care to keep a tight lid on the

investigation, restricting access to information, keeping status strictly need-to-know but he didn't ask Harwick how he knew about the mole or doubt that it was true. If Harwick said it, it was fact. "What do you know?"

Harwick took another drag on the cigarette then crushed it against the doorframe with a lot more force than was necessary to extinguish it. "Nothing. No face. No name. All I know is that our mole exists."

Harwick's anger was palpable. Mitch could well relate. There were only a handful of people working the Rossington case, and Mitch had selected each one of them. The mole could only be someone he knew. He tamped down on his rage for the moment. First things first. "What about you? How's your cover?"

"Solid. They're bringing me in deeper every day. Local business man, my ass." Harwick sneered. "Fuck, Mitch, this guy is into everything dirty and depraved." Harwick's lips thinned. "I want to nail Rossington by his balls."

Yeah, Mitch wanted that badly. "We'll get him, Dan."

Harwick gave one swift nod.

"I'll be in touch," Mitch said.

"What are you going to do about the mole?"

A rush of anger heated Mitch's face. "I'm going to find that bastard."

* * *

A 911 call would bring the police. Shelby couldn't let that happen. She couldn't let the police find the messenger. If her association with the messenger and the man who sent him was discovered ... she couldn't let herself think about the consequences of that without losing her mind.

As she sucked air into her starved lungs, she scrambled for a reason to stop Joseph but fear had numbed her ability to think and before she could come up with an excuse, Joseph had made the call.

She had to get out of here before the police arrived. Again, she tried to gain her feet but her arms and legs felt as strong as overcooked noodles.

"Should you be movin' around, Dr. Grant? Better to stay put, I think," Joseph said. "You should stay put till the ambulance gets here."

"I don't need an ambulance." Her throat burned from the messenger's choke hold on her neck and her voice came out raspy, belying her statement.

Deep crevices cut into Joseph's brow and his eyes narrowed in concern behind wire-rim glasses. But when Shelby continued to struggle, Joseph grasped her arm. "Here let me help you, Dr. Grant."

Joseph hovered at her side as she ignored pain in her middle where the messenger had squeezed her, and made her way from the alley and back to the street. Her purse and briefcase were in front of the clinic where she'd dropped them. Shelby bit back a moan of pain and bent to snatch up the items. She dug inside for her cell phone. Her hands were shaking so badly the phone slipped in her grasp. She let out a whimper of frustration and fear, then locked her fingers around the phone and sent a text message. One asterisk. The man who'd sent the messenger to her tonight had devised a single star as their signal to meet.

He had to meet with her tonight—now. She had to assuage the anger that had prompted him to send her this warning. She squeezed her eyes shut. She had to drive home the depth of her commitment to him. Though how he could doubt that, doubt her ...

Shelby opened her eyes and stared at the phone, willing to see an asterisk in response. Praying to see one. Seconds ticked by and the screen remained dark.

Tick. Tock.

Fear filled her and a scream began to build. She bit her lip hard to suppress it, breaking the skin and tasting blood.

"Dr. Grant, you want to call someone?" Joseph said. "The Chief? You're shaking something awful and no wonder at all. Here, let me call Chief Turner for you."

Calling the man she was engaged to marry would be the normal thing to do, but Mitch was the last person she wanted to see now.

"No!" In her anxiety, in her panic, the word erupted from her before she could stop it. Joseph's frown deepened at her vehemence. She swallowed and tried to think, tried to sound sane. She pushed hair back from her face. The strands were damp with perspiration brought on by fear. "No need to call Mitch, Joseph. No need to worry him." She swallowed. "I just—just want to put this behind me and go home." Though his intervention had done her more harm than good, she couldn't discount that Joseph had put himself in harm's way for her. There hadn't been many people in her life who would do that. Ignoring her stinging palms, where bits of gravel had cut into them when she'd landed on the ground in the alley, she reached out and clasped Joseph's arthritic hand. "Thank you. Thank you for everything you did tonight."

Joseph ducked his head and mumbled something but she didn't catch the words. Her attention became riveted on an ambulance and the patrol car right behind it that turned onto the street.

Both vehicles screeched to a halt at the curb, sirens blaring, roof lights flashing. Neighborhood residents, no doubt alerted by the wailing sirens, poked their heads out their front doors. Some left the confines of their homes to stand on their lawns and peer across the street while others ventured nearer, taking up positions on the chipped sidewalk and the brown grass in front of the clinic.

A cop and a medic exited their respective vehicles and began closing the distance to Shelby. She didn't want a report of this incident. She needed to send both the medic and the cop on their way.

As the men reached her, and she was about to do just that, a black SUV she knew all too well pulled in behind the cop car. The driver's side door was flung open and before the SUV had rocked to a stop, Mitch charged out. Her stomach clenched then dropped.

Mitch was dark-haired and tall with a hard, tough body. Standing above those around him, his eyes, a deep penetrating blue, landed on her. He kept his gaze trained on her as he made his way through the men and women that blocked his path to her.

Shelby tilted her head back to continue to look at him as he stopped in front of her. "I thought you'd be home by now."

Was she going into shock? Of all the things to say to him, that had to be the most inane. Mitch must have thought so as well because his gaze on her intensified.

"Had a meeting," he said softly.

He still wore the charcoal-gray suit he'd had on when he'd left for the police station that morning, though the tie was no longer knotted and hung loose on his crisp white shirt. The jacket was open, showing his paddle holster and cell phone on either side of his belt.

His brows were low, his handsome face pulled taut with worry. He lifted a hand to her neck and his gaze hardened. It was obvious by his expression that the skin there was marked. So much for keeping what had happened today from him. Her struggle with the messenger had left marks on her that she would never have been able to hide from Mitch.

Despite the look in his eyes that was now lethal, Mitch wrapped his arms gently around her and drew her against his body. "Are you hurt anywhere else? Did he—"

She didn't need to clarify what he was asking.

KAREN FENECH

She shook her head quickly, hastening to reassure him, of this, at least, and ease his fear. "No."

Mitch's hold on her tightened. She ignored the pain in her middle made worse by his fierce grip and wound her arms around him. For just this moment, she gave in to her need for him. Allowed herself the delusion that she was safe. That she wasn't alone. That what she had with Mitch was real.

He held her for a long time. She let him hold her far longer than she should have, undermining her intention to show him that what happened tonight was not as significant as he believed it was. It was significant, all right. Just not for the reasons Mitch thought.

Finally, he pressed his lips to her brow. He drew back slightly, just enough that he could look at her. "Have you been examined, honey?"

"Just got here myself, sir," the medic said.

Mitch rubbed his hands up and down her arms, left bare by the sleeveless pale blue dress she wore. Goose bumps had pebbled her skin. He removed his suit jacket and placed it around her. When he tried to pry her cell phone from her cold fingers, Shelby held tighter. If Mitch wondered about her strange attachment to the phone, he didn't press the issue and let her continue to hold it. With one arm around her, he gently led her to the ambulance.

There was no point denying the medic now. Any hope she'd had of keeping the attack from Mitch was long gone. She'd only draw more attention from him if she didn't allow the medic to examine her neck and to treat her abraded palms.

After, she declined riding on to the hospital for a more thorough examination. Mitch didn't look pleased with that. "Honey, you should be seen by a doctor."

Shelby shook her head. "That's not necessary."

At her hoarse voice, his eyes narrowed. He looked about to make a stronger case for a hospital visit then released a breath and let the matter drop. He received instructions from the medic on what to watch for that would suggest a complication from the trauma she'd sustained to her neck, then led her to his vehicle. He positioned her with her side against the passenger seat and with her feet on the running board. Leaving the door open, he stood in front of her. He ran his thumb along her cheek. "What happened tonight?"

Shelby closed her eyes.

"Take your time."

He thought she needed time to fight back the trauma of being attacked before she could respond. While that would certainly be believable, what she needed time for was to decide what to tell him. How much to tell him. His touch was gentle, so tender, tears welled in her eyes.

Mitch brought her close again. "Easy, baby. Take it slow."

Her hands were against his chest, her fingers curled around his shirt. She forced herself to release him and brought her hands together in a tight grip. "There isn't much to tell." She cleared her raw throat carefully. "I was leaving the clinic and a man came up behind me."

Mitch's body tensed though his arms around her remained gentle. "Take me through it."

His tone was calm but his eyes were fierce. His gaze remained on hers and fearing that her own gaze was too open just now, she lowered it to her hands. She gave him an edited accounting of the incident, leaving out that the man had spoken to her and what he'd said. She didn't want to mention Joseph but couldn't see a way out of that. Mitch was sure to find out about Joseph and would consider the man a witness. Fear of what Joseph may have seen made the fine hairs on the back of her neck rise. "Jo-seph called out," she went on, "and the man who held me released me and ran a-way. I was in the wrong place at the wrong time." She needed Mitch to believe that.

He didn't respond to that but asked instead, "Did you get a look at him?"

"Too dark and he was behind me the entire time." That, at least, was the truth.

Mitch rubbed her shoulder. "Okay. Don't worry about that. There are other ways to find this bastard."

Shelby's throat tightened. "I just want it to be over."

She didn't want Mitch pursuing this but how to deter him? Any logical woman—logical person—would want a violent man off the streets for their own peace of mind as well as to prevent him from hurting anyone else. Added to that, she was a psychologist who counseled survivors of violence. She saw up close how violence devastated lives and had dedicated her career to helping her patients overcome such trauma and resuming their lives. Dealing with violence—living with violence—weren't foreign to her. She'd known all about the shattering effects of violence long before she'd met any of her patients.

"Chief? Dr. Grant?" Joseph said.

Joseph and Mitch were acquainted from times Mitch had stopped by the clinic to see Shelby.

Mitch kept one arm around Shelby as he turned to greet Joseph. Mitch held out his hand. "Mr. Bowden. Thank you."

Joseph shook Mitch's hand. "I didn't do anything, Chief. I'm just glad I picked that moment to take out the trash." Joseph shifted position, shuffling his feet in his brown polished shoes. "I overheard you sayin', Dr. Grant, that you were in the wrong place at the wrong time, like the attack was random. I'm not so sure about that."

If you'd like to know when the next Protectors novel is released, sign up for Karen Fenech's notification-only newsletter at her website: www.karenfenech.com Go to the "Contact" page and scroll down to the last listing on that page for the option to subscribe.

Originally Released In Hardcover
Coming To Paperback Soon
Available Now As An eBook

UNHOLY ANGELS

Liz Janssen's marriage was over long before she filed for divorce. There was no way her soon-to-be ex-husband committed suicide because of her. Yet that is what her teenage son, Will, believes.

Others in the small West Virginia town share this thinking. Others who are disciples of a homicidal Satanic cult her husband was part of. The disciples want vengeance for the death of one of their own and will use Liz's troubled, grief-stricken son as an instrument for their revenge.

To save herself and Will, Liz must stop them - and she must do so without Doug finding out.Doug McBride is the new town sheriff, the man Liz has fallen in love with, and the man she cannot trust.

Please note: Some content may be disturbing.

Originally Released In Hardcover
Also Now Available As An eBook

BETRAYAL

To save her son and people from a deadly enemy,
Lady Katherine Stanfield marries her former
betrothed, a man she'd betrayed but has never
stopped loving. Katherine has never revealed her
reason for the betrayal and now, five years later,
believes her secret is safe.

But someone won't let the past rest. Someone
with a secret of his own. She must stop that
"someone" because he wants Katherine and her
new husband dead.

ABOUT THE AUTHOR

PRAISE FOR THE NOVELS OF KAREN FENECH

{GONE} Karen Fenech's GONE is a real page turner front to back. You won't be able to put this one down!" —NEW YORK TIMES BESTSELLING AUTHOR KAT MARTIN

{GONE} "Karen Fenech tells a taut tale with great characters and lots of twists. This is a writer you need to read." —USA TODAY BESTSELLING AUTHOR MAUREEN CHILD

{GONE} Readers will find themselves in the grip of GONE as this riveting tale plays out. GONE is a provocative thriller filled with a roller coaster ride that carries the suspense until the last page." —DEBORAH C. JACKSON, ROMANCE REVIEWS TODAY

{BETRAYAL} "An excellent read." —DONNA M. BROWN, ROMANTIC TIMES MAGAZINE

{IMPOSTER: The Protectors Series - Book One} "IMPOSTER is romantic suspense at its best!" —USA TODAY BESTSELLING AUTHOR MAUREEN CHILD

{UNHOLY ANGELS} "... a superbly intricate tale of greed, power, and murder... a suspenseful and believable story that will keep you reading into the wee hours of the morning. Highly recommended! —BESTSELLING AUTHOR D.B. HENSON

Karen Fenech lives with her husband and daughter. To find out more, visit her website at: http://www.karenfenech.com

If you'd like to know when the next Protectors novel is released, sign up for Karen Fenech's notification-only newsletter. Go to the "Contact" page at www.karenfenech.com and scroll down to the last listing on that page for the option to subscribe.

Made in the USA
Coppell, TX
21 April 2024

31541349R00138